KU-377-352

Pierre Audemars has written another novel featuring M. Pinaud, of the Sûreté, of whom it has been said "a perfectly credible, sympathetic even impressive comic detective". The story opens with Pinaud finding the first headless corpse purely by chance. This bizarre discovery leads him to the strange family at the Château Capt and to the remote town of Chassagne where he is met by more violent deaths. His investigations and his eventual solution to a diabolical mystery make an arresting story rich in originality and excitement.

To my nephew
PAUL

A CONSUL BOOK

THE FIRE
AND THE CLAY

PIERRE AUDEMARS

WORLD DISTRIBUTORS   LONDON

A CONSUL BOOK

This CONSUL edition, complete and unabridged,
published in England, 1961, by
WORLD DISTRIBUTORS (MANCHESTER) LTD.,
36, GREAT RUSSELL STREET, LONDON, W.C.1.

Copyright © 1959 Pierre Audemars

Text set in 10 on 12 point Times

Printed and made in Great Britain by
The Racecourse Press Limited
23 Coleridge Street, Hove 3, Sussex.

Chapter One

IN the days when M. Pinaud's fame had grown to such as extent that no one ever dared to question his veracity, he never grew tired of repeating the astounding story of the headless corpses.

"Great events," he would declare, surveying his audience through clouds of cigarette smoke, "from little causes grow. So it was in this case. And yet how I became involved was extraordinary. You would never believe it."

His audience believed everything, and swallowed the aphorism. Who were they to argue with the greatest detective in France? Besides, when M. Pinaud was speaking, there was nothing else to do, except to listen.

It happened that M. Pinaud was driving the wife of M. le Chef back from a function whose importance had been sufficient to warrant her attendance, to a town which has no importance at all, since they never arrived there.

Actually, the wife of M. le Chef has no importance in the story at all, but her importance to M. Pinaud was considerable, in view of the fact that although in his own estimation he was undoubtedly at this time the greatest detective in France—M. le Chef was still his employer. So considerable that his anxiety and his distress became understandable.

It is essential—if one is to understand M. Pinaud's aphorism—that one should attach their relative importance to the various events of that memorable evening.

In the first place, why M. Pinaud should have been detailed to drive the wife of M. le Chef anywhere is a matter which the chronicler has never attempted to make clear and in any case has no importance whatever. The fact that M. Pinaud—whose appreciation of good wine was far superior to his ability to gratify it—did more than justice to each and every bottle as soon as it was opened is a fact of far greater importance. And the fact that the countryside through which they were passing was singularly bleak and desolate, without so much as a bush or a tree or a shrub or a haystack which would have afforded the necessary cover—that too, is important.

And the wife of M. le Chef—she too, was extremely important. Her opinion as to one's behaviour—even in the most trying of circumstances—would no doubt carry considerable weight when it came to a question of adjudicating merit for promotion. . . .

M. Pinaud drove faster and faster, his rapid glances from side to side becoming increasingly desperate.

He was too much of a realist to regret having accepted M. le Chef's suggestion with smiling alacrity; after all, when one has a career to make, one does not argue with one's employer. But none the less he would not have been human had he not wished that M. le Chef had brought his son or his nephew or his uncle or even his grandfather to the function, instead of his wife.

With a man beside him the situation would not even have arisen. Between men, there is no false modesty. With a man another man can always arrange himself. With a woman, things immediately become more difficult, more complex.

M. Pinaud may not have come from a wealthy family, but nevertheless he had been brought up in a correct manner. There are certain things which are done and certain things, on the other hand, which are definitely not done. At least, not in the presence of a woman.

Now for M. Pinaud to realize this and to remember such things no doubt did him credit and reflected well on his upbringing, but one can understand and sympathize with him in the realization that they brought him no comfort, neither did such thoughts mitigate his distress.

For a long time the road had followed the railway line. Now they began to climb and the gleaming rails sank and disappeared into a cutting. A low blue and white signpost announced a road junction and M. Pinaud thankfully applied the brake in anticipation. The side road joined the main road over a bridge, and as they reached it M. Pinaud was out of the car almost before it had stopped.

His apology and excuses to the wife of M. le Chef were a model of propriety and eloquence, but unfortunately their effect was rather lost in that the greater part was delivered, clearly and concisely, as M. Pinaud was scrambling down the side of the cutting beneath the bridge.

The autumn evening had been a beautiful one, tranquil and calm.

Now the last lingering veils of that loveliness grew shadowed and dim as the dark fingers of twilight enfolded the sky like a shroud. The translucent peace seemed to linger even as it died, even as the shadows spread, even while the darkness hesitated as if reluctant, as if fearful at the memory of a brightness too brilliant to banish.

M. Pinaud sighed with a great and profound satisfaction.

Then he caught sight of the body on the line, almost indistinguishable in the deeper shadow cast by the bridge.

Without hesitation he scrambled down to the line. The

body was sprawled out in the gloom, with its neck and what had been its hands on the rail. The head was on the track a few yards away.

M. Pinaud remembered the train that had passed him as though he were standing still and wondered if he were going to be sick.

He forced himself to light a cigarette, although his shaking hands could hardly manipulate his lighter. For a few moments he stood there motionless, lost in thought, inhaling smoke with a kind of abstracted determination.

Men had been known to commit suicide by this method, although there were undeniably easier and less unpleasant methods of dying. The place had been well chosen; the shadow cast by the bridge practically concealed the body. The time, too, was appropriate: the half-hour of twilight before the engine's headlamp would be switched on.

And yet—and yet—for a suicide there was remarkably little blood.

Again, not only the site but the locality had been well chosen; the line ran perfectly straight for a hundred kilometres. This was where the *grande rapides* all made up time. At such speeds an engine driver concentrated on the signals ahead and the temperature of his bearings rather than on the blur of the track which was being swallowed up in front of him almost faster than his eyes could follow. Besides, if there was anything on the track, that was just too bad. At that speed there was nothing to be done.

M. Pinaud knew all this. He knew, too, that normally the body would have remained there undiscovered until the morning, by which time it might have rained and the blood, it would be assumed, had been washed away.

For a long moment he remained there, impassively smoking, contemplating the horror in front of him with

8

unseeing eyes, his mind camly and logically reviewing the situation.

Then, suddenly, he threw away his cigarette. Bending low, he gathered up the body powerfully and easily, and carrying it in his arms as one would a sleeping child, made his way back to the road and his car.

Although the twilight was deepening, there was still enough light for the wife of M. le Chef to distinguish M. Pinaud's gruesome burden.

She gave one piercing shriek and slid quietly down the seat in a dead faint.

M. Pinaud cursed his tactlessness, his thoughtlessness and his lack of consideration—all those very same qualities on which he had been congratulating himself such a short time ago.

Of what use had been his forbearance, his *savoir faire* and his delicacy for those long and uncomfortable kilometres, if all the credit he had thereby gained had now been destroyed? He should have warned her—prepared her for the dreadful shock.

But it was no use crying over spilt milk. Having exhausted his vocabulary, M. Pinaud sighed philosophically. He had work to do. M. le Chef would be the first to agree.

He opened the boot with one hand and put the body inside. Then he went back for the head.

Then he wiped his hands on one of Madame Pinaud's discarded and yet still beautifully soft undergarments which she had thoughtfully put in the car as a duster and inserted his bulk behind the steering wheel. The wife of M. le Chef had not moved.

M. Pinaud threw her a glance of infuriated concern as

he started the engine and let in the clutch. As if he did not have enough on his mind already, without the added complication of a fainting woman.

He drove rapidly through the gathering dust, switching on his headlights after a short while and scanning the countryside anxiously for some signs of human habitation.

At length, coming in from a side road, a low stone wall began to run parallel to the road. A wall meant an estate, and an estate a house, and a house meant people and a telephone and smelling-salts for the wife of M. le Chef.

M. Pinaud sighed with relief and trod on the accelerator. But the wall just went on, kilometre after kilometre, with woods and fields on either side, empty and dark and deserted. M. Pinaud continued to sigh, but now with exasperation, as that interminable wall showed no signs of ending.

Then his headlights picked out a van, drawn up by the side of the road, and M. Pinaud applied his brakes skilfully and hard and drew up beside it. A gigantic figure in stained and greasy overalls straightened itself with a heavy jack held lightly and easily in two immense hands.

"Trouble?" asked M. Pinaud easily.

"Oh no—thank you, m'sieu. Only a puncture——"

The man's voice broke off abruptly as he caught sight of the inanimate figure on the front seat.

"It's all right," said M. Pinaud hastily. "You need not look at me like that—I am neither a white-slaver nor a kidnapper. This lady has fainted, as you can see. I am looking for a house. That is why I stopped to ask you."

"Well, there is the Château further up the road—this is the wall of the estate . ."

"I know—I have been following it for hours."

"It is an extensive property, m'sieu," the man agreed. "But nothing now to what it used to be."

"Well, how much further?"

"Only a few kilometres up the road. There is a gatehouse, but it is no longer used. The gate is open—drive straight up . . ."

"And in three hours I ought to come to the Château?"

The man's swarthy features were suddenly transfigured by a charming smile.

"No—it is not as bad as that. The house is quite near the road."

"Good—and the town?"

"Chassagne—another five kilometres."

"Thank you. I am obliged to you."

"It is nothing."

Darkness had fallen by the time M. Pinaud drew up outside the Château. Even with the light which shone above the high front door he could distinguish little more than a massive rectangle of grey and weatherbeaten stone.

He switched off the engine and climbed the steep flight of stone steps which mounted, unusually, parrallel and not at right angles to the wall, to the level of the great carved front door.

He pulled the iron-handled bell and waited while its soft echoes died. After a long time there came the sound of slow footsteps and then the door opened.

An elderly woman regarded him with a severe and forbidding countenance.

"It is much too late to call," she told him. For a moment M. Pinaud felt at a loss. But only for a moment.

"Good evening," he replied, politely and cheerfully. "I

would not dream of disputing the truth of your statement. Unfortunately, I am a victim of circumstances——".

"Whoever you are," she interrupted even more severely, "You ought to know that it is much too late to call."

"I know it is late," he agreed, still with great politeness. "But this is an emergency——"

"What is it, Victoire?" interrupted another voice.

M. Pinaud already held his hat in his hand. At the sight of the newcomer he bowed, quite naturally and with great dignity. She was so beautiful that he felt it was the least he could do.

Two large eyes stared at him from the exquisite oval of features that were far too pale to be healthy, and a slender hand played nervously with the locket at her throat.

"I was telling the gentleman, mam'zelle, that it is much too late to call——"

"And I was endeavouring to explain, mademoiselle," M. Pinaud interrupted swiftly, "That this is not a social call, but a matter of some emergency. I have a lady in my car who has fainted, and I came to ask if perhaps you would have some smelling-salts or a restorative."

"But of course—we shall be only too pleased to help. Can you bring her into the house? She will be more comfortable on a sofa than in your car. Don't stand there gaping, Victoire—give m'sieu a hand."

"Thank you, mademoiselle," said M. Pinaud, "You are very kind. I can manage to bring her inside, if you would be good enough to show me the way."

The grim-faced Victoire held open the door of the car while M. Pinaud lifted out the inanimate body of his employer's wife. It took a far greater effort, he reflected, than carrying the headless corpse up from the railway line, and when at last, after negotiating innumerable stone passages, countless unexpected and uneven steps and a huge banqueting hall, he finally laid his burden down on a sofa, it was with a thankful sigh of relief.

"And what, may I ask," declared a beautifully modulated and yet extremely imperious voice, "is the meaning of all this?"

M. Pinaud then realized that the room into which he had been shown already had an occupant.

This one had to be the girl's mother—their features had been cast from the same mould—but this one was like an eagle, proud and arrogant and haughty. This one swept down on him with regal condescension, and in the proud and fierce old eyes there flashed a spirit that was like fire.

One could imagine that exquisitely modulated voice hardening until it cut like a whip and stung like a lash, and at the same time one felt its richness and tenderness and all its vibrant awareness. Beside her, the girl's loveliness was a pallid mask. Beside that fierce pride, the girl's face was dead.

M. Pinaud sensed all this in a flash, for his was an acutely perceptive nature, and he wondered, since wondering at incongruity was his trade, but his heavy features remained impassive as he bent to arrange the skirt in a more decorous fashion about the legs of the wife of M. le Chef.

"This is my mother, Madame Capt, m'sieu——"

The girl's voice was mechanical, disinterested, as though she were thinking of something else.

M. Pinaud bowed.

"My name is Pinaud," he replied. "Forgive me for intruding in this way, but this lady has fainted from shock."

"So I can see."

The touch of an acid reproof sharpened the music of the modulated tones.

"But why bring her here?"

M. Pinaud kept his own voice flat and expressionless as he replied.

"I was driving her in my car to the house of friends when it happened. I brought her to the nearest house, madame, which was yours."

For a moment there was silence. Then the old lady inclined her head.

"I see. Marie, fetch the smelling-salts on my dressing-table."

When the girl had left, the old lady continued to eye M. Pinaud with fixed severity. He bore her scrutiny unmoved and looked around at the room with interest.

It was beautifully and luxuriously furnished in a style of two generations ago, with hand-embroidered cushions on the plush-covered settee and armchairs and a wrought-iron stone, set in a tiled recess, that was a veritable work of art. The longcase clock in the corner was a collector's piece, and the walls were covered with pencil etchings and framed photographs. It was a beautiful room, with a character and a harmony all its own.

"What I cannot understand, m'sieu," M. Pinaud heard the beautifully modulated tones saying, "is how a lady travelling in a car could have suffered a shock severe enough to make her faint."

The words in themselves were innocent enough, but their implication was plain—that M. Pinaud was a philanderer of the lowest type.

Now this implication was more than unfair, since one had only to look at M. Pinaud with his burly and rugged

features, his cheap and badly fitting suit, and his service-
able and square-toed boots, to realize that not only was
such an implication unfair but that also it must necessarily
be completely unfounded, since whatever M. Pinaud's
faults, they were hardly conducive of a mentality or a
nature likely to express themselves in shocking females
to the point of fainting . . .

M. Pinaud was only human. Perhaps it was this un-
fairness which prompted his reply.

"It is really quite simple, madame," he said quickly and
quietly. "I found a body without a head on the railway
line and carried it back to my car."

The reaction to his words was completely unexpected.
The old lady went as white as a sheet and tottered to
the nearest chair, where she sat down heavily and stared
in front of her with tragic, unseeing eyes.

A noise from the door distracted M. Pinaud's attention from this interesting development, and he looked up
in time to see the bottle of smelling-salts rolling on the
carpet and the girl framed in the doorway, her eyes dark
pools of horror, her hand held to her mouth as if stifling
a scream.

And then, for a moment, there was silence.

M. Pinaud walked to the door, stooped and retrieved
the bottle of smelling-salts.

"So you see," he continued blandly and expression-
lessly, "it is hardly surprising that she fainted. After all
it is not the sort of thing one encounters every day."

There was no answer. He drew the stopper from the
bottle and held it under the nostrils of the inanimate
figure on the sofa.

Then the old lady spoke from the chair. Her voice was slow and heavy and filled with an unutterable weariness.

"You will forgive us, I am sure, m'sieu. I am suffering from an abscess behind the ear-drum which causes me sudden pangs of intolerable pain. My daughter, too, is not well—she is at present under treatment by Dr. Reuge. Please excuse us if our behaviour appears wanting in courtesy."

The apology was adequate, even gracious. M. Pinaud realized what an effort it must have cost her pride. And yet the atmosphere of constraint was there—thick and palpable and inexplicable, as tangible as a physical presence.

M. Pinaud continued to move the bottle slowly to and fro, his features impassive, his mind racing at a furious speed.

"Perhaps a cloth with cold water, mademoiselle," he suggested gently, more to break the tension than anything else, since the wife of M. le Chef was already beginning to move.

"Of course," the girl whispered and disappeared. In a moment she was back with a cloth and a bowl of cold water.

With a cold compress on her brow and the aromatic vapour in her nostrils, the wife of M. le Chef soon recovered and sat up and demanded to know what all this was about.

M. Pinaud apologized profusely.

"I am so sorry, madame, but you fainted in the car. . . ."

"Oh yes—it was dreadful—why on earth did you bring such a thing——"

"It was necessary, madame," M. Pinaud replied gravely.

16

"I had no choice. I came across this body on the railway line. The fact must be reported to the proper authorities."

"Yes, I suppose so. But wouldn't it have been simpler to have left it there and pretend that you never saw it?"

"Very much simpler," agreed M. Pinaud with a tolerant smile. "For one who is the wife of M'sieu le Chef," he added beneath his breath. Aloud he continued:

"But even the normal citizen has his obligations. In my official capacity I have more."

He did not miss Madame Capt's sudden start, although he kept his eyes apparently on the wife of M. le Chef.

"Yes—I suppose you are right. But where are we now?"

"I had no means of reviving you, madame," M. Pinaud told her. "And so I drove you to the nearest house, where Madame Capt and her daughter were kind enough to receive you and do everything possible to help."

The wife of M. le Chef smiled with considerable charm. Not for nothing had M. le Chef achieved his present position of eminence—a position, his detractors were apt to maintain, to which a bachelor would never have been able to attain.

"I am deeply indebted to you both," she murmured graciously, "for your hospitality as well as your kindness."

The old lady made a great effort. Her smile was a triumph of self-control.

"We were only too pleased at the opportunity to help," she said pleasantly, "although it is M'sieu Pinaud you should thank, rather than us. You were in good hands, madame."

M. Pinaud bowed to acknowledge the compliment. He wondered what the daughter Marie was thinking. He wondered what lay behind those enigmatic dark eyes

17

which were watching him with such unseeing intensity. He wondered at the atmosphere of fear and constraint which seemed to fill the room with the threat of its hostility—an atmosphere to whose strangeness and intensity he was particularly susceptible because of that very normality which constituted his character.

But nothing of what he wondered revealed itself on his impassive countenance. He replaced the stopper in the bottle and held out his hand.

"Well, madame," he said, "if you feel that you have sufficiently recovered, we should be on our way. It is getting late."

As they came down the steps M. Pinaud saw that the lid of the boot was wide open. Crouched underneath, someone was examining its contents with great interest.

Behind him, M. Pinaud heard the old lady catch her breath. Almost in the same instant she called out clearly:

"Roland!"

The figure straightened and stood upright beside the car. By the light which hung above the front door M. Pinaud saw the figure of a man, young and slender, clad in a spotlessly white shirt and an old pair of flannel trousers. His hair appeared to be blond, but as M. Pinaud walked towards the car he saw that it was prematurely white, in strange contrast to the youthful delicacy of his features.

"This is my son, Roland," whispered the old lady. Perhaps M. Pinaud was the only one there who realized what it had cost her to speak.

The young man's eyes, he noticed, had been curiously vacant in their lack of expression. Now, as he heard her voice, they suddenly seemed to melt with tenderness, transfiguring his features in a remarkable way.

"Yes, Mother," he said dutifully.

After the introductions had been completed, he turned to M. Pinaud with a strange eagerness.

"You carry luggage of a remarkable nature, m'sieu?"

M. Pinaud eyed him thoughtfully.

"Yes," he agreed slowly. "You seem to be interested——"

"I am—I am. I saw many like that in the war——"

"Roland . . ."

Again the word was hardly more than a whisper, but at the very first syllable the eager voice ceased abruptly and again he looked at her with the same almost intense tenderness and again he said dutifully:

"Yes, Mother."

The noise of an engine was heard, increasing rapidly in volume. As they stood there waiting, twin pencils of light from the headlamps moved rapidly up the drive.

M. Pinaud felt a hand on his arm. Turning, he saw that Marie Capt was standing close to him.

"I must speak to you," she whispered. "Will you be staying in Chassagne?"

Her words were barely audible above the noise of the approaching engine, but there was no mistaking their urgent and almost desperate appeal.

M. Pinaud bent closer.

"Yes—I must make my report. Come to the hotel tomorrow."

"Thank you."

Suddenly they were all bathed in light. The engine spluttered and died as the van turned in a half-circle and came to a stop. Even before the gigantic figure climbed out from the driver's seat M. Pinaud recognized the van as the one he had passed before on the road.

The driver walked to the back and heaved up the sliding door. Reaching inside, he pulled out a large basket which he set on his shoulder.

"Good evening, Madame Capt," he bawled cheerfully, "I have brought your meat."

For a moment there was silence. Before anyone could speak M. Pinaud opened his mouth.

"Surely," he remarked without any particular emphasis, "it is rather late to be delivering meat?"

"Granted, m'sieu. I am not usually as late as this. But then I had a puncture—as you will remember. You are the gentleman who asked me the way to the Château, are you not? I thought I recognized your car."

"Yes," agreed M. Pinaud. "And I recognized your van."

"You should—it is the same one. And how is madame."

"I am quite recovered, thank you, m'sieu," remarked the wife of M. le Chef in the kind of tone that implied precisely it was about time all this idle chatter ceased and people were allowed to depart in peace.

"Good—good," said the butcher cheerfully. "Shall I take it in, Madame Capt?"

There was no answer. The man clattered up the stairs with his basket on his shoulder. M. Pinaud murmured his thanks and his farewells and shepherded the wife of M. le Chef into the front seat. Then he started his engine, switched on his own powerful headlights and manœuvred the car skilfully as he turned so that their brilliant light shone into the open back of the van.

It was empty. Two iron rails ran along the roof, one each side; from them hung several large and powerful meat-hooks. As the car moved on, M. Pinaud noted the name painted on the side of the van:

ROSTAND, CHASSAGNE.

And as he accelerated down the drive he was thinking that if anyone should ever wish to transport a headless corpse to a railway line, a butcher's van would be the ideal means of locomotion to choose. The dark stains he remembered on the man's white overalls must have been blood. A little more or less would never be noticed.

Chapter Two

AND so the wife of M. le Chef passes, finally and irrevocably, from out of our story.

Whether she ever commended M. Pinaud's behaviour on the night in question is not known, and indeed—if one takes the trouble to peruse all the volumes of the great man's celebrated Memoirs, in which not one but a hundred proofs of his unique and outstanding ability are convincingly and methodically chronicled—it is not even important. M. Pinaud needed no praise, neither did he pay any heed to blame, in his swift and meteoric rise to fame.

Behold him, then, on the following morning, seated in the office of M. le Commissaire Minoton and in the august presence of M. le Maire.

M. le Commissaire was long and lean, with a harassed parchment face and gifted with an almost poetic eloquence. M. le Maire, as befitted the most important *vigneron* in the district, was stout and dignified and prosperous.

"Now the most interesting thing about this affair, M'sieu Pinaud," declared M. le Commissaire, "is that it has happened before."

M. Pinaud stiffened like a hound on the scent.

"Indeed?"

"Yes. Three days ago a man was found dead in the garden of the Château."

"You mean in the Château of Madame Capt?"

"Yes, m'sieu. That is the only Château here."

"I see. That explains many things I could not understand. But please forgive me—continue."

"A dead man, as I said, was found in their garden. A man, irrevocably dead—since his head, neatly and completely severed, obviously with one blow, lay several metres away from the body—and yet unmistakably recognizable."

M. le Commissaire seemed to take comfort not only from the echoes of his own voice but also from the respectful silence about him, and continued with even greater confidence.

"Recognizable as a man who had lived all his life in this town of Chassagne, and loved and drank and argued and quarrelled—particularly with Rostand the butcher— and used the name of Jean Falange. But that does not really matter. He will not use it any more. Neither will he quarrel as he used to, since he would find that difficult, without a head."

"Undoubtedly," put in M. le Maire aggressively. "But keep to the facts, man."

Some of M. le Commissaire's confidence evaporated, but he was soon in his stride again.

"Beside the headless trunk were the tips of eight fingers. Eight fingers. The first or index, the second, the third and the little fingers, duplicated, or of each hand. This added to the confusion. I made notes at the time, which confirm these facts numerically, but do nothing to dispel the confusion. The finger-tips belonged to the hands of Jean Falange. I myself, not without a great effort but conquering my natural repugnance with thoughts of a richly deserved promotion, fitted them on. Just to make sure. The index tip on the index finger, the second tip on the —but why go on? It is useless. This, I said to myself, was more than a crime, a criminal assault, a murder. This was madness."

M. Pinaud stirred heavily in his chair. This was interesting. M. le Maire strode up and down restlessly.

"It is the facts, M'sieu le Commissaire, in which M'sieu Pinaud is interested," he declared.

With commendable presence of mind M. le Commissaire quickly and skilfully altered the first word he had been about to say.

"The tips of these fingers had been severed with a force and a precision comparable to that which had removed the head of Jean Falange from the body of Jean Falange. This fact, logically and inevitably, caused me to think immediately of a butcher's cleaver. A butcher's cleaver, by association of ideas, brought me to Rostand the butcher, with whom the dead man had been known to quarrel, violently and bitterly. And then M'sieu le Maire intervened and impeded the course of justice."

M. Pinaud looked at M. le Maire with interest. M. le Commissaire looked at him as well, reproachfully. Under the influence of their combined stares, M. le Maire ceased his restless pacing and proceeded to justify himself.

23

"I said—as far as I can remember," he declaimed judicially, "something like this: Consider, M'sieu le Commissaire—consider well before you act rashly and hastily and with imprudence. Granted that these two were always quarrelling—but then Rostand the butcher has quarrelled at one time or another with everyone in Chassagne. He is a quarrelsome man. Also he is lonely, since he has no living relatives. We all know that. But that does not necessarily make him a murderer.

"Granted also that these mutilations could have been made with a butcher's cleaver. Indeed, barring a very sharp axe, it is difficult to think of any other weapon. But you yourself examined the head. The features were composed, without injury. Dr. Reuge examined the body. There was no trace of poison or drug or excess of wine, no mark of violence.

"Did Jean Falange, then, stretch out his neck and wait meekly for his head to be severed? Did Rostand invite him to lean conveniently over his bench, beside a leg of pork? Nonsense. You know what a temper the man had. It is ridiculous."

"It is more than ridiculous," agreed M. le Commissaire gloomily. "As I said, it is madness."

M. Pinaud lit a cigarette and puffed out clouds of smoke in absorbed abstraction.

"You know," he said slowly and thoughtfully, "I am inclined to agree. But what you have told me is very interesting."

The door opened and a white-clad figure entered the room. Dr. Reuge was tall and well-built, with a beautifully trimmed beard and a merry twinkle in his shrewd brown eyes. His voice was resonant and amazingly powerful.

"Gentlemen," he began, "I hope I am not intruding—but you told me to report as soon as I had finished. This suicide——"

"Which is not a suicide," put in M. Pinaud calmly.

Dr. Reuge stared. Then he laughed, shortly and hardly.

"Which, as you say, m'sieu . . , m'sieu . . ."

"This gentleman is M'sieu Pinaud, from the *Sûreté*," said M. le Commissaire. "M'sieu Reuge is our doctor and police surgeon."

The two gentlemen bowed politely to each other.

"M'sieu le Docteur."

"M'sieu Pinaud—as you say, which is not a suicide."

Suddenly the twinkle died from the brown eyes and they narrowed, staring at M. Pinaud shrewdly and appraisingly.

"Why do you say that, m'sieu?"

M. Pinaud met his regard levelly.

"Supposing you tell us. After all, you are the police surgeon."

The twinkle returned and the doctor laughed.

"Quite right. Easy enough. The incision on the head does not correspond to that made by the wheel on the neck. One cannot judge from the hands, but the very fact that they were placed on the rail suggests that the fingertips were already missing. I should say he was killed in the same way as Jean Falange, and a very clumsy attempt made to conceal the fact as a suicide."

M. Pinaud nodded.

"Yes—I agree. And also the question of the blood—or rather, the lack of blood. There was not enough. But then I found the body unexpectedly, soon after the train had passed. Normally, it would not have been discovered until

25

the morning. As you say, a clumsy attempt—the efforts of an amateur. Any other points?"

"No. No marks or means of indentification on the clothing. From their state and the amount of dirt I should say he was a tramp."

"No fingerprints, of course," put in M. le Commissaire. "I wonder if that was the object of cutting off the finger-tips. . . ."

"You forget that they were left beside the body of Jean Falange," put in M. le Maire in his turn with an acid emphasis, "and also that in his case everyone knew who he was."

"True," agreed M. le Commissaire dejectedly. "The more one thinks about it, the madder it becomes."

M. Pinaud was not listening. He had been thinking. Now he looked again at Dr. Reuge.

"No marks of violence?"

"No—although about that it is difficult to be dogmatic. There were bruises on the head, where it was probably moved violently by the impact of the train, but these may have occurred after death. No signs of drugs or poison or anything abnormal in the organs. No papers in the pockets."

"I see. Well, we shall take over from here. Let us have all this information in your report."

"Certainly, m'sieu. Will you be wanting me for anything else?"

M. Pinaud glanced at M. le Commissaire, who sighed and shook his head.

"No, thank you, M'sieu le Docteur."

"I must be going too," announced M le Maire. "Glad to have met you, M'sieu Pinaud. You will do what you

26

can to help us, won't you? This is a dreadful thing—a terrible thing for Chassagne."

"I will do my best, m'sieu," replied M. Pinaud. "Therefore you need not worry."

"What do you mean? I do worry. Why do you say I need not worry?"

"Because now you have Pinaud looking after everything. And Pinaud has promised to do his best," M. Pinaud reminded him gently. "Here in Chassagne that may mean nothing to you. Elsewhere M'sieu Pinaud's best is usually sufficient."

M. le Maire stared, muttered something and went out with the doctor. When the two men had left the room, M. Pinaud became aware that M. le Commissaire was regarding him with an air of grave concern.

For a moment he ignored him, fumbling in his pocket for his cigarette case and lighter and making a great show of lighting a cigarette, but beneath the unwinking intensity of that reproachful scrutiny he grew restless and irritable.

"Well?" he snapped at length. "I had to tell him something, didn't I?"

All the pent-up feelings of M. le Commissaire now exploded in a stream and a torrent of words.

"Yes, but you did not have to tell him that. There was no need to raise his hopes—you spoke as if the case were solved. Solved—how can it be solved when it cannot even be understood?

"Here we have two dead bodies, without heads. One found in a garden, one on the railway line. They may be connected; they may have nothing to do with each other. One we knew, one we don't know. In every crime there must be a motive—where are the motives here? What is the point of these murders? Are we up against a fanatic—a madman?"

As suddenly as he had begun he stopped. Then he stood up and walked to the window, where he stood, staring out with an intensity which obviously saw nothing.

"You are quite right," agreed M. Pinaud gently. "Nevertheless, what I said was true. I have every confidence in my own abilities. I have not failed yet. This one is difficult, and will therefore take a little longer."

For a moment there was silence, and then suddenly M. le Commissaire spoke without turning his head.

"Have you ever seen a man guillotined?"

M. Pinaud stared.

"No—have you?"

"Yes—once. I shall never forget it."

"Why did you mention it?"

"I just suddenly had an idea."

"What was it?"

M. le Commissaire turned from the window and faced him.

"I would rather not say—not at the moment."

For a moment M. Pinaud felt angry. This was a fine way to behave—this was a fine example of how not to collaborate. Was this to be another instance of provincial resentment at the *Sûreté's* interference? Besides, how on earth was he going to solve this case if ideas were withheld from him? At the present moment he had none of his own, which made it all the more infuriating.

But another look at that lean and harassed figure standing there so respectfully and so nervously before him melted his wrath like mist on a summer's morning. After all, he could afford to be magnanimous. He was Pinaud. He had arrived. He could afford to feel compassion for those who had as far to go. He knew, better than most, the difficulties and the dangers that lay in the path of achievement.

And so his voice was gentle as he spoke.

"Could it have something to do with our two corpses?"

"It might be. The effect would be the same. But I will let you know very shortly, once I have verified my suspicions."

"Very well. In the meantime, set everything in motion to try to discover the identity of this second one—you know, the usual routine—Bureau of Missing Persons, detailed physical description and all that sort of thing. You might get a report from Dr. Reuge on the state of the mouth and get the Bureau to circulate the dentists."

"It shall be done, m'sieu."

"Good—oh, and another thing, although I suppose this is pretty useless. Dig up everything you can on Jean Falange and his private life. There might be a motive somewhere."

"We have already tried that one, m'sieu—I am afraid it is hopeless. But we are still questioning as many as we can of the people who knew him, in the hope of finding out something."

"Good—that is the only way. Keep on and on—something always turns up. I will see you later. Perhaps we could take a glass of wine together. I am going to call on Rostand the butcher."

And so M. Pinaud, practising with admirable thoroughness that philosophy which he preached to others, kept on and on until he found himself in the shop of Rostand the butcher.

In this case he proved himself a false, prophet, since

nothing turned up, and when he left, being a man who was always singularly honest with himself, he could not have said with any conviction that he had made very much progress.

But then if M. Pinaud had allowed himself to become discouraged by every reverse and setback he had experienced in the course of his astonishingly memorable career, it is quite definite that he would never have achieved such outstanding success.

In his memoirs he points out, with engaging candour, that perhaps it was because he found himself so often wrong that in the end it became a simple matter of perseverance to prove himself right.

This quite remarkable statement is worth studying, as it reveals an interesting aspect of his character. The doubts, the uncertainties, the failures, the humiliations, the weariness, sometimes the utter despair—all these are not mentioned, which surely is a fact of some significance, since there is no doubt that M. Pinaud experienced more than his share. And yet he could dismiss them and ignore them; his vision saw beyond them.

And now he stood in the shop of Rostand the butcher, watching with a kind of horrified fascination as the gigantic figure brought a cleaver down with a force sufficient to split the massive bench and neatly severed a huge joint of beef.

"Aha, it is M'sieu Pinaud."

"How do you know my name?" M. Pinaud countered swiftly.

The butcher grinned.

"News travels fast in a small town," he replied coolly. "Especially bad news," he added sardonically.

30

M. Pinaud did not say anything. The butcher lifted his cleaver again.

"I mean the bad news about the body, of course," he said, and smashed the cleaver down again with a force that set the iron hooks shivering on their bars above his head.

"I would be extremely obliged," said M. Pinaud slowly, "if you would be kind enough to stop doing that for a few moments while I ask you some questions."

"Certainly. Would you care to come into the office?"

"No, thank you. This will not take long. Last night when I commented on the unusual hour you choose for delivering meat, you told me that you had been delayed by a puncture."

"That is quite true, m'sieu—you yourself saw me changing the wheel."

"I also saw that your van was pointing away from the Château and not in the direction of delivering meat."

M. Pinaud's voice was quite expressionless. His regard, too, was blandly inquiring, and yet for a moment Rostand sensed an inflexibility of purpose that was as hard as steel and he looked down at the patient burly figure in front of him with a new respect.

"That is also quite true, m'sieu. I was so eager to see an acquaintance of mine in the village of Moudon that I forgot all about the meat. Normally it would not have taken long, but I had trouble getting the wheel off. One of the nuts had rusted and jammed."

"And what did you do?"

Still the quiet voice was without expression, but a film of moisture appeared on the butcher's upper lip.

"I tried putting oil on it and waiting, but that had no

31

effect. In the end I lost patience and forced it—or rather I tore the bolt in half since the nut would not give. The broken bolt is still on the wheel, m'sieu."

"And where is this village of Moudon?"

"You take the side road at the end of the estate, where the wall turns. A kilometre down the road."

"And the name of your acquaintance?"

"Madame Reymond. She is a widow."

"I see."

"May I ask the purpose of these questions, m'sieu? Am I suspect?"

"Everyone is suspect, M'sieu Rostand—until the mystery is solved. Everyone in Chassagne is, in my eyes, a potential murderer—until I arrest the real one. That is why I am asking you questions. Thank you for answering them so frankly. Do you know anything about the other body, that of Jean Falange?"

"No—except that I found him."

"Oh—indeed? That I did not know. So you were the one who found him. Where?"

"In the garden of the Château."

"How? When? Tell me all about it."

"Well, there is nothing much to tell, m'sieu. Three days ago—it was early in the morning. I just saw it lying there as I got out of the van."

"Where was the head?"

"Just beside it."

"Did you move anything, touch anything?"

"No. I told Madame Capt and we telephoned M'sieu le Commissaire."

"Was there a lot of blood?"

The butcher put up a gigantic hand and scratched his head.

"I don't really remember, m'sieu. It was lying on the grass and there had been a heavy dew. I don't seem to remember any at all, but it might have soaked in."

For a moment there was silence. M. Pinaud stood there frowning, lost in thought.

The door opened slowly and a small and solemn girl entered the shop and walked straight past him to the bench.

"Please, M'sieu Rostand—here in this match-box is the piece of wood we found in the last sausage and *maman* says she expects a substantial reduction in the price of this new one I have been sent to buy on account of the wood which we could not show you actually embedded within the sausage as we ate the sausage all of us being hungry."

M. Pinaud, still frowning, went out.

The butcher's story was plausible and would probably —almost certainly—stand up to confirmation. Otherwise he would not have been such a fool as to tell it. And yet . . . and yet . . . the sight of that cleaver, wielded with such powerful ferocity, had been strangely disturbing.

It was not an easy thing to sever a man's head cleanly, with one blow.

"The majority of murders," declared M. Pinaud didactically, swallowing his wine appreciatively, "are committed because of a motive."

M. le Commissaire, seated opposite him at the café table, raised his glass and sipped his own, and managed to convey even in that simple action an unutterable anxiety that the whole thing might blow up in his face. He nodded with a gentle courtesy that somehow seemed only to add to his air of perpetual concern.

"That is quite true," he agreed politely.

M. Pinaud looked gratified. It was not often that he had such an attentive audience.

"The principal motives," he continued, grasping the carafe and re-filling his glass, "are love, fear, and greed, and their subsidiary or ancillary motives. These are the three basic urges which lead to murder."

"Yes," agreed M. Minoton thoughtfully. "I suppose any motive could be finally classified under one of those three headings."

"Precisely. The taking of a human life, which is a sacred thing, in normal circumstances—and by that I mean not in time of war—is an extreme and primitive action which needs the motification and primitive urge which must be equally as strong. The instinct of sex, with all its ramifications of love and jealousy and thwarted desire; the instinct of fear, with which is allied self-preservation; and the instinct of greed or acquisition—these are the three base motives which inspire the majority of mankind's endeavour, and which are therefore strong enough to justify, apparently, the taking of a human life."

After listening to the sound of his own voice throughout this masterly disquisition, M. Pinaud considered that he had earned another drink.

He lifted the carafe and looked at M. Minoton, but that worthy held up his hand firmly. Apart from the one sip, his glass stood untouched before him. His worried features were alive with interest as he leaned forward over the table.

"You said the majority——", he began.

34

"Yes," agreed M. Pinaud. "That is why, sooner or later, we usually catch the murderer. Once we have the motive, most of our work is done. But sometimes we come up against the apparently motiveless murder—and that is where it becomes difficult. We have occasionally the person who kills for no apparent reason—the maniac who kills for the pleasure of killing, or the psychopath who kills to satisfy some perverted desire.

"That is when we find it hard. If someone who—through some sexual aberration—hates all prostitutes, chooses to go around sticking a knife in them, I can assure you that it is more than likely he will never be caught. Imagine the task of the police in such circumstances."

M. Minoton looked suitably horrified, more perhaps at the choice of subject than its implication. M. Pinaud watched him shrewdly.

"Now in our case," he continued smoothly, "we have what are apparently two motiveless crimes. I say apparently, because they may be motiveless to us for the simple reason that we do not know the motive. We have Jean Falange as the first victim. As far as you have been able to find out, no one had any motive for killing him. And we have this unknown tramp—if Dr. Reuge is right—as the second victim. Did anyone have any motive for killing him? And are these two murders connected in any way?"

Here M. Pinaud paused to take breath. He had been looking severely at M. Minoton. Now he eyed the carafe of wine with a benign approval, noting that at the present rate of M. Minoton's consumption its contents would provide him with several more glasses.

M. Minoton stirred uneasily is his chair. One would have said, to contemplate these two, that M. Pinaud was interrogating a murderer, and not drinking with a colleague. But then M. Minoton was that type. His shoulders carried the sins of the world. Now he contemplated his glass as if the problem of emptying it had become insoluble.

"It is all very difficult," he murmured.

Once again M. Pinaud looked at him shrewdly.

"Therefore it will take us a little longer," he stated cheerfully.

But beneath his cheerful appearance his mind was working keenly and logically. Before, M. Minoton had been eloquent and assured; puzzled certainly and perhaps confused by the mystery of the crime, but nevertheless, in his own mild and diffident manner, competent and alert. Now he was abstracted and worried. It was obvious that he was thinking of something else.

M. Pinaud poured himself another glass of wine.

"M'sieu Minoton," he said quietly, "you have a suspicion."

M. Minoton started guiltily.

"Er—yes. Well—in a way . . ."

"M'sieu Minoton, I think you should tell me your suspicion. After all, we are working on this case together. I am a frank and truthful man. Other and lesser men would perhaps rest on their laurels and boast without justification. But not Pinaud. I confess I am just as puzzled and just as mystified as you are. I need your help. I need your collaboration."

M. Minoton was so gratified by this confession—which, coming from M. Pinaud of the *Sûreté*, was not to be lightly discounted—that he actually lifted his glass and took another sip of wine. But even as he set the glass carefully down, the expression on that worried countenance told M. Pinaud that he had lost.

"I would like to, M'sieu Pinaud. I can assure you there is nothing I would like better. But not at this stage."

"But why not?"

"I do not feel that it would be fair."

"To whom? To the murderer?"

"No—no—of course not. To—to the people concerned. You see, I may be completely wrong."

"But you may be right. I should think you are not often wrong."

"Thank you, M'sieu Pinaud. In that case I will tell you—tomorrow morning—or in a day or two. . . ."

"But why not now?"

"No—no. I have no proof. I just had an idea—which may be completely wrong."

M. Pinaud contemplated his glass moodily. It was useless. There is nothing more obstinate than a mild and diffident character when he is firmly convinced that he is right.

The situation was galling, to put it mildly.

Here was M. Minoton, who suspected someone or something and who would therefore approach the problem in his own cautious and old-fashioned way and who could not be persuaded to make a definite statement until he was convinced that his suspicions were justified—and here was Pinaud, the shining light of the *Sûreté*, the most famous asd celebrated detective in France, the solver of a hundred complex and baffling crimes, stuck here in this provincial town without a clue, without an idea, without the first thought as to how to proceed.

"And I thought that first I should make a preliminary investigation . . ."

M. Minoton's voice droned on, but M. Pinaud hardly troubled to listen. What was the point? That was the difficulty with these conscientious types—they always saw the other person's point of view. To succeed in this jungle, a man should only see his own.

"Because, after all, should the verification of my suspicion prove it to be unfounded . ."

M. Pinaud grasped the carafe firmly in one hand and his empty glass in the other. For a moment, not unreasonably, he thought of breaking them over M. Minoton's head, but his exasperation was only momentary and vanished even as it came. M. Minoton was a good and conscientious man, and only trying to do his duty.

Besides, it was good wine, and paid for. It would be a pity to waste it.

With the wine warm in his belly, glowing through his veins and expanding in his consciousness, M. Pinaud changed hs mind and ordered another carafe.

After all, there came a time in every case, however difficult, however complex, when it was wise to sit back and relax and try to visualize the problem as a whole.

The lightning perception, the intuitive deduction, the flash of genius—all these qualities which singled out certain individuals from the common herd of detectives —these were all very well and had to be employed, continually and with skill, at the beginning and at the end, but in the middle sometimes it was far better to relax and think things over quietly and reflectively in order to see where one was going.

Besides, it was excellent wine and cheap, and the chair was comfortable, and the mellow autumn sunshine was comforting and—since he always remained a realist—M.

Pinaud honestly and truthfully knew that at this stage there was not very much else that he could do.

"Tell me," he said, leaning forward as far as his bulk permitted, "tell me about these people at the Château whom I met last night. I find them interesting."

"They are interesting," agreed M. Minoton, averting his eyes with an expression of relief from the sight of the new carafe. "The old lady is quite a character. You know that she can trace her descent from Hugues Capet?"

M. Pinaud remembered the pride in the fierce old eyes and nodded his head slowly.

"That does not surprise me at all."

"During the Occupation she was never worried—the Château never touched. She went to see the local Commandant. The story goes that he ended up by standing to attention in front of her."

M. Pinaud laughed.

"That too, I can well imagine."

"She is well loved. That family is part of Chassagne. There has always been a Capt at the Château—it is just one of those things, like the church and the market square.

"And the son?"

M. Minoton sighed.

"Ah, that is a tragedy," he said slowly.

M. Pinaud gestured towards the carafe. M. Minoton did not even see him. His eyes were turned inwards. For a long moment he sat there in silence, while M. Pinaud waited sympathetically.

"There was a fine young man," he continued at length, "indeed, those two were children to be proud of—he and his sister. We were all proud of them, as if they had been our own. And he was brave in the war, as brave as a lion. Some of the men here in Chassagne served in his regiment. They will tell you—he did not know the meaning of fear. It takes courage to stand up to a dive-bomber with a machine-gun and to get near enough to a tank to stick an iron bar in its tracks. With more like him France would never have been beaten. And then he was wounded—in the head."

M. Minoton sighed and absent-mindedly drank from his glass, without realizing, M. Pinaud was perfectly sure, what he was doing.

Then he set the glass down, still without seeing it, and his eyes, filled with kindness and compassion, looked at M. Pinaud.

"You have seem him?" he asked gently.

"Yes," replied M. Pinaud. "I saw him last night."

The echoes of his words seemed to hand in the air after he had spoken. M. Minoton left them. They carried their own answer. There was no need to elaborate.

Then M. Pinaud stirred in his chair.

"And the daughter—Marie?"

"She has changed. She is no longer the same person. Perhaps it is not surprising."

M. Pinaud frowned.

"No. The old lady sees what she wants to see. The girl is young—she would see it all."

"Yes. It is a great pity."

Again, for a moment, there was silence. Then M. Minoton moved uneasily in his chair.

"If you will forgive me, M'sieu Pinaud, but I have so much to do."

"What—oh yes, of course. I am so sorry. Do not let me detain you."

When he had gone M. Pinaud remained perfectly still in his chair for a long time He stared at the glass which

M. Minoton had left half-full, but he did not see it. His thoughts were chaotic and confused and yet continually, unendingly active.

He remembered all his impressions of the night before. Coldly and methodically he remembered each incident, each inflection of speech, each word that had been said. And from these ordered recollections the thoughts came to fly off as if in the mad confusion of a revolving catherine-wheel.

There had been a very strange atmosphere in that place. It might be an interesting family, but it was also a very strange one. And the first body had been found in their grounds. Was that the reason for the strangeness, or was there something more?

It was all very confusing. M. Pinaud eyed the new carafe of wine on the table with a sudden completely objective severity and then he did a strange thing.

"Garçon," he bellowed in a stentorias voice.

The waiter came at the double.

"M'sieu?"

"See that carafe of wine?"

"Yes, m'sieu—is there anything wrong?"

"No. It is excellent wine. You have not been paid for it yet—here. Take this."

"Thank you, m'sieu."

"And take that wine and drink it."

"But . . ."

"It is good wine and, as you have just observed, it is paid for. Drink it. Enjoy it. And be thankful. I am only sorry I cannot join you."

"But why not, m'sieu?"

"No. I have problems. I am beginning to think that I have landed in the middle of a very strange business.

There may be a time for serious drinking, but it is certainly not now. Good day to you."

And M. Pinaud levered himself up from his chair, clapped on his hat and left the café.

Chapter Three

THERE is only one hotel in Chassagne, a fifteenth-century building of historic interest and considerable charm. M. Pinaud found the beams and the panelling more interesting than the visage of Dubois the innkeeper, a shifty-eyed individual whose surliness matched his un-prepossessing appearance; but as it was the only place available M. Pinaud sighed philosophically, bought some pyjamas, a razor and a toothbrush, telephoned Paris to have his suitcase dispatched and booked a room.

As he returned to the hotel now, the proprietor was waiting for him in the entrance hall.

"Mam'selle Capt is waiting to see you, m'sieu," he announced. "She is in the lounge—that door there."

"Thank you," said M. Pinaud, and opening the door without hesitation, entered the room, thankful that he had limited himself to one carafe of wine.

Marie Capt was sitting motionless in an armchair, staring at the wall with a strained intensity.

A shaft of sunlight through the ancient blown glass of the window illuminated her features and touched her hair with a golden haze, and again M. Pinaud marvelled at the wonder of her beauty. Yet he felt that it was the beauty of a statue. Because of her pallor, and the strained and rigid intensity of her expression, her features had a classic perfection that was immobile and frozen. He wondered, even as he watched her with a grave absorption, what could have driven the life and the happiness and the animation from her features, and suddenly he knew, with a swift sudden surge of emotion, that whoever witnessed the return of these things would see a loveliness miraculous in its wonder.

His voice was very gentle as he spoke.

"You wished to see me, mademoiselle?"

With a start she turned her head. Her hands, which had been clasped in her lap, parted, and she stood up. M. Pinaud noticed that she wore a magnificent engagement ring, a large solitaire diamond of the finest quality.

"Oh! M'sieu Pinaud—yes. I don't know what you thought of me last night asking if I could see you—but I can't stand it any longer—that horror in our garden and now another one. . . ."

M. Pinaud reached out and took her hands and guided her gently but firmly back to the chair.

"Now, mademoiselle," he said quietly, "just sit down and relax. I will do all I can to help you. But you must tell me all about it—truthfully and from the beginning. There—that is better. Just sit there quietly for a moment and then tell me what is wrong."

M. Pinaud could be very soothing when he wished. The girl relaxed visibly, and when she began to speak her voice was quiet and normal and no longer hysterical.

"You ask me what is wrong. It would be simpler and shorter to tell you what is not wrong. Everything seems to be under some sort of curse since the war. Before, I can remember the happiness that seemed to envelop the Château like a lovely shining cloud. Now everything has gone wrong. First of all we had the trouble with Roland."

"What trouble?"

M. Pinaud's question was swift, and yet his voice was still gentle—gentle and quiet and soothing so that the words seemed to glide quietly in and take their place naturally beside the thoughts the girl was speaking aloud. Her train of thought was not disturbed and she answered as if without realizing that she had been asked a question.

"He was badly wounded—in the head. For a long time he was in hospital; they would not discharge him. It nearly broke my mother's heart. For two years she drove herself to the point of collapse and spent money like water to get him out."

And she succeeded?"

Again that gentle prompting evoked an unhesitating answer.

"Yes, she succeeded, but at what a cost. She is the ghost of her former self. And now she has all the worry and the responsibility—and when he is bad the torment of wondering if she has done the right thing, or whether it would have been better to have left him in the hospital."

"Is he often bad?"

"No, not often. Very seldom, really. But then the wound is opened, and all the heartbreak and the agony she endured begins again. He is the heir, you see—the last of the Capts."

M. Pinaud remembered the pride that dominated every line of the old lady's features and nodded his head in silent agreement.

"Then, when I was engaged I became ill—I who had never known a day's illness in my life. I became ill with an illness which no one can diagnose—which has no pain and no symptoms, but just kills all the life inside me——"

With incredible speed M. Pinaud reached out and his

large hand grasped the two slender ones clasped together. He sat on the arm of her chair and his other hand went around her shoulder in a gesture that was friendly and comforting and infinitely soothing.

He did not speak, but the girl's voice, which had been rising once again to the point of hysteria, suddenly checked and ceased at the physical contact, and for a while they sat there in a silence that was complete in its understanding.

"Illnesses can be cured you know," he said after a while.

The girl laughed hopelessly.

"Mine can't."

"Rubbish."

"That is what I would have said—a long time ago."

"You will say it again, I promise you."

"Oh—if only I could!"

There was such heartbreak in her voice that M. Pinaud —without really knowing why and without confidence or justification—found himself repeating the words he had just said.

"I promise you."

Then again there was silence between them as they each sat there, together and yet alone with their thoughts. And yet in that silence there was no constraint. M. Pinaud was not aware that it existed. In his mind there was no silence, only the reverberations of innumerable unanswered questions. To Marie Capt it was a silence of peace and understanding, and when at last she looked up and broke it there were tears of thankfulness in her eyes.

"Thank you, M'sieu Pinaud, you have given me hope again."

"Tell me, mademoiselle, who is your fiancé?"

"Dr. Reuge. You met him this morning. He has taken me to hospitals and clinics and there have been consultations with other doctors and diagnoses and opinions, until I am sick of the whole thing—oh, and that reminds me, it is time for my pills. Would you be kind enough to ring for some water?"

When the water came, M. Pinaud watched her gravely while she took a phial from her handbag and extracted two small white pills. Sipping a little water, she swallowed them with a dexterity born of long practise.

"What are they for, mademoiselle?"

"Oh—just a sedative, or so Armand told me. Something to relax me, because I am so strung up."

M. Pinaud frowned.

"I do not believe in pills," he declared.

"Neither do I. But I am ill, so I do what I am told. After all, he is the doctor."

"Yes, I suppose so. But in my day young girls did not take pills—except for a specific reason, and then they never had any effect. Fresh air and exercise, and sound sleep at night—these things do more good than pills out of a tube."

Marie Capt stared straight at him and through him.

"I am supposed to be quiet after taking them," she said slowly and gravely.

M. Pinaud stood up.

"Very well. Rest here for a few moments while I go and get my car. I will drive you back to the Château. I would like to have a few words with madame your mother."

M. Pinaud was aware of the strain in the old lady's

eyes as she faced him proudly, and his voice was gentle as he spoke to her.

"Madame Capt, I am sorry that I have to disturb you, but there are a few questions . . ."

"About the body?"

"No, although I can understand how you were upset last night. I did not know about the first one."

"It was horrible."

"That I can well believe. Have you any ideas?"

"Ideas? Of course I have ideas—or rather, one idea. It must have been Rostand the butcher."

M. Pinaud spread his hand deprecatingly.

"But one must have proof——" he began.

"Proof—nonsense! One does not need proof. Go and look at the man's vile countenance—that is proof enough."

"It would hardly carry weight in a court of law, madame. Besides, even assuming that Rostand did it—and we still do not know how—why should he put the body in your garden? We can presume that it was taken there from the scene of the crime, because of the absence of blood."

"That is easy," rejoined Madame Capt composedly. "He did that to injure me and to throw suspicion on me."

"Indeed? And why should he want to do that?"

"Because he is an upstart. Because he hates me as much as that other upstart, the Mayor. They can never forgive me for the fact that my ancestors lived in this Château when theirs were living half-naked in a hovel. If it was not Rostand then it was the other one, the Mayor."

"And what has he got against you, madame?"

A flush slowly stained the broad whiteness of madame's brow, but her lovely lilting voice did not falter.

"I am in his debt. It cost me a fortune to get Roland back, and another fortune to keep him here. I had to borrow money from him."

The brave unfaltering voice ceased, but it was as if that pride it had killed surged again, renascent, in the poise of her head. M. Pisaud waited, and his silence was more sympathetic than any words. In a moment she continued.

"I would rather die than sell or mortgage the Château or any part of our estate, and so I had to borrow. Now he will not give me a moment's peace. He does not want the money back—he knows I have not got it—instead he is trying to get me out. The Château is immensely valuable and the revenue from the estate is considerable, but to raise ready money takes time in an agricultural district. That is why he is pressing me."

For a moment there was silence. Then M. Pinaud sighed.

"All this may be true, madame, and yet in view of the evidence it is difficult to attach the blame to either of them. There is no proof. And why cut off the finger-tips?"

"That I do not know. I can only say that there must be a reason to else it would not have been done."

M. Pinaud contemplated her with a new interest. Actually, this was the first sensible thing she had said. If only he knew the answer to that one he would have solved the problem.

"It is all very difficult," he said slowly, "but as a matter of fact, I did not come here to talk about the crime. That is my problem—mine and M'sieu Minoton's. There is so need for you to worry or concern yourself with such a thing; we shall solve it eventually. No, my questions were to have been about your son Roland."

Something seemed to die in the keen old eyes and yet the regal poise of her head did not alter.

"Yes, m'sieu?"

Her voice was perfectly steady, without a tremor, and yet M. Pinaud could sense what an effort it had cost her.

"Perhaps it would be better," he suggested gently, "if I did not ask any questions at all, but you just tell me about him."

"Thank you, m'sieu, for your forbearance and your understanding. He was badly wounded in the head—and over a year in hospital. They would not discharge him. Apparently he had periods when . . . when . . ."

For a moment her voice faltered. Again M. Pinaud could not but admire her courage as she fought for self-control.

"That is quite a common occurrence," he said matter-of-factly, "with head-wounds."

She looked at him gratefully.

"Yes, if they are bad enough. In the end I got my way. I still maintain I acted for the best. You have seen him. You can judge for yourself. When—when it does happen —I am with him. He is at home, surrounded by those who love him. We can look after him. At least he is happy. In the hospital his heart was breaking."

Suddenly she pressed a hand to her ear, stood up abruptly and walked to the window.

"Here he is happy. He has a workshop and a forge. He is very clever with his hands. I remember the day he was awarded his *baccalaureat* . . ."

Her voice ceased suddenly and she came back to sit down.

"Forgive me, m'sieu, sometimes the pain in my ear is more than I can bear. Sometimes when I am with

Roland I think that there are not four horsemen of the Apocalypse, but five. The fifth is far more terrible than the others, because his name can hardly be put into words. My son Roland is one of his victims—and there are so many others. Have you ever seen any of them, m'sieu?"

"Yes," agreed M. Pinaud gravely. "I know what you mean."

"The unfaithful wives and husbands and the children forced to grow up without love or control—so many evil consequences from a simple thing like a broken home— the old people left without their sons and daughters to an old age that can only be lonely and bitter—perhaps compared to these horrors mine is not too great. I have only to watch a gifted and brilliant engineer working with his hands like a mechanic and a blacksmith and accept the fact that he is quite happy doing it."

For a moment her iron self-control wavered, but indomitably she fought for mastery, refusing to give in.

M. Pinaud watched her with respect and compassion and kindness, and then went out and left her alone, shutting the door quietly behind him.

Before, when he had driven Marie Capt from the hotel, he had been too preoccupied to pay any attention to his surroundings.

Now he stood in the sunlight and seemed to see the Château for the first time, a lovely rectangle of massive and weatherbeaten stone, dignified with age, with a vast sloping roof of lead tiles which seemed to ripple like the sea under the hot bright glare of the sun.

The front of the building, apart from the worn stone steps which led down from the door, presented a strange blankness, due to the fact that the whole lower part was nothing but huge and massive stones for a third of its height. The level of the living-room was well above his head as he stood there for a moment, frowning with absorbed interest, his mind still hearing the old lady's beautifully modulated voice.

Then he went around to the back, where the outbuildings enclosed a garden, blazing even at this late season with a riot of colour. Here the back of the building was warm and alive with contrast; a balcony projected under a gaily-striped sun-blind with boxes of flowers set in its weatherbeaten beams.

Rows of windows, framed in their white-painted shutters, relieved the bareness of the ancient stone and revealed an extent and a size which the magnificent proportions successfully concealed. It was a strangely original house, and a very beautiful one—and yet suddenly M. Pinaud shivered, as if with cold.

Then he sighed and made his way towards the outbuildings. In one, which had once been a barn, he found Roland.

One end of the building had been fitted up as a workshop, with a forge and anvil, a bench, a vice, a lathe and racks of tools. Most of the floor space was occupied by an enormous Bugatti car, whose bonnet had been completely removed. Bending over the exposed engine was the white-haired figure of the old lady's son.

M. Pinaud came to lean over the other side in a companionable silence. Roland looked up, nodded and smiled, and went on with what he was doing. After a while M. Pinaud took out a cigarette and spent a long time lighting it.

"I wondered where these had gone," he said at length. "He only made a few—six, was it?"

"Ten."

Roland looked up again as he answered. M. Pinaud noticed that his eyes were alive and sparkling with intelligence and animation. His own lit up as he contemplated the huge and intricate mechanism of the engine, each and every part burnished with the meticulous finish of a fine quality watch.

"What an engine. Is it yours?"

"No. I wish it were. It belongs to Dr. Reuge. We work on it together, but now he is busy, and so I am looking after it for him."

"What is the trouble?"

"Oh, there is no trouble with an engine like this—apart from the fact that it is practically impossible to run it at the revolutions for which it was designed. Hence the plugs have always got to be cleaned."

"I wish I could drive it," said M. Pinaud wistfully. Roland laughed.

"You must ask Dr. Reuge," he replied. "It is quite an experience, I can assure you."

For a moment there was silence, while the barn seemed to sleep in the heat of the sun. Roland worked on busily. M. Pinaud smoked in a contemplative silence.

Then Roland laid down his box-spanner and feeler-gauge and looked up, in his eyes a curious dead emptiness that sent a shiver down M. Pinaud's spine.

"Did you—want anything, m'sieu?"

With an almost physical effort M. Pinaud looked away from that vacant stare and down at the engine.

"Nothing much, just a question. You seemed very interested in that corpse last night. You said you had seen many in the war——"

"I did. I did."

Roland wiped his hands on a piece of cloth and walked around the front of the car to stand beside M. Pinaud.

"You would never believe it—but it happened. I saw it. There were three men, standing in line, beside me. I don't know why they should have been standing like that—there was no reason—it was just one of those things. We were not expecting anything at the moment, but one of their tanks came down the road well ahead of schedule. That was the trouble, they were always ahead of schedule. No one seemed able to believe that they would make such superhuman efforts.

"It was a shell from that tank. One moment those three men were standing beside me, and the next moment—incredibly—they were still standing there—without any heads. I tell you, m'sieu—they stood there—without any heads. Three bodies—three corpses—without any heads——"

M. Pinaud reached out and grasped his arm.

"Easy, now—easy," he said soothingly. "That was a bad one, but it is all over now."

The vacant emptiness was still there, but behind it there was a glow—a light of madness all the more horrible for the film of emptiness it could not pierce.

"Yes," agreed Roland slowly after a pause, "it is all over now, but it was not over then—not for a long time. Not for all the time they stood there beside me—without heads. It seemed hours—it can't have been long—but it seemed hours. It was long enough for me to remember them today—and to see them today, just as I saw them at that moment. Then the blood came and they fell down. But that was a long time after."

For a long moment, after the slow tense voice had ceased, there was silence.

M. Pinaud did not break it. He retained his grasp on Roland's arm, and stood there rock-like, matter-of-factly, letting that silence with all its hideous memories flow over him and around him and past him, while he continued to stand there, as if defying it—an ordinary man, a normal man, a figure typical of the sanity and decency that had replaced and outlived and triumphed over that time of violence and bloodshed and horror.

And when at last he spoke, when he felt the trembling flesh beneath his fingers quieten, his voice, too, was quiet and normal and matter-of-fact.

"Yes, these things are bad to remember—and yet you should be proud to remember them. You were the one chosen to endure them. You bore that burden—not of your own choice, but for the sake of others. Yours was the sacrifice—yours should be the pride."

Roland laughed, hardly and bitterly.

"Pride? In what? In the wasted years—in the nightmares in hospitals—in the acceptance of a life like this?"

And he flung out his arms in a gesture that was pitifully tragic. Then his voice changed and softened, and its intensity was almost more than M. Pinaud could bear.

"Pride—in what I see in my mother's eyes whenever she looks at me? No, m'sieu, I think you have chosen the wrong word."

"Nevertheless," replied M. Pinaud quietly, "I do not think that I am wrong. Perhaps I expressed myself badly. But the very fact that I tried to express myself at all should help you to understand, if you think about what I said."

And he went out of the barn and made his way back to his car.

Chapter Four

THAT evening M. Pinaud went up to his room at the hotel, washed, and then lay down on the bed, smoking a cigarette. He tried to sort things out in his mind, but after a while he came to the conclusion that there was really nothing to sort out, nothing tangible, no concrete fact, only a number of vague impressions which nevertheless troubled him, perhaps because of their very inconclusiveness.

M. Pinaud sighed and got up. Tidily he brushed all the cigarette-ash from the bed and put out the butt in an ash-tray. Then he opened the door and went in search of the dining-room.

He did not have to ask where it was. He could smell the steak he had ordered from the top of the landing.

As soon as he had sat down a plump young girl brought in the meal, and Dubois, the innkeeper, appeared with a bottle of wine in his hand.

"M'sieu Pinaud," he said, "I have here a remarkable Mercurey which I am sure you will be delighted to try."

M. Pinaud, his knife and fork already in his hands, looked up with a gratified smile.

"That is extremely civil of you, m'sieu," he replied courteously. "I am very partial to Mercurey."

"You may have drunk Mercurey before," said Dubois, "but you have never tasted anything like this."

He uncorked the bottle carefully and poured the wine reverently. M. Pinaud noticed that the man's eyes were bloodshot and restless—the eyes of an inveterate drinker, and he wondered what could have prompted the invitation, but he continued to eat unhurriedly and then waved his hand.

"Bring a glass and join me," he said.

"Thank you, m'sieu."

They drank. M. Pinaud savoured the fragrant *bouquet* of the wine on his tongue and then sipped a little slowly, feeling a glow rising and expanding within him like a warm and friendly hand, comforting him, reassuring him with strength and wisdom and courage. It was a remarkable wine. It was a wine before whose brilliance the shadows of fear and poverty and futility and failure melted. It was a wine that surged and mounted within a man and inspired him and made him immortal, filling him by a divine illusion with all the qualities with which he had never been born.

Over the rim of his glass he regarded the innkeeper steadily. After a moment the man's restless bloodshot eyes wavered and looked away. M. Pinaud set his glass down carefully. In the very innermost recesses of his mind some sixth sense rang a warning bell, very softly, very faintly, and yet very definitely.

"You are right," he declared with the utmost gravity. "Never before have I tasted anything like this. It is magnificent—beyond description."

The innkeeper emptied his glass.

"I keep this wine," he said solemnly, "for those who appreciate it. Their number grows smaller each year. The world is not what it was."

"I quite agree. May I ask you to bring another bottle?"

"Certainly, m'sieu."

And he went off, presumably to the cellar. As soon as he was alone, M. Pinaud grasped the bottle and looked swiftly around the room. On either side of the old-fashioned fireplace stood two huge plants, their pots concealed in elaborately chased brass urns.

With a speed almost unbelievable in a man of his bulk, M. Pinaud was out of his chair. It was the work of a moment to pour most of the contents of the bottle into one of the urns, and when the innkeeper returned, he was seated once more at the table, masticating his steak with a benevolent and paternal air.

He waved his knife cheerfully and pointed to his wineglass, which was full.

"I am sorry," he said with painstakingly careful articulation, "and I regret—but you have been such a long time —and this steak is so tender. I am afraid you will find that bottle empty."

The innkeeper's shrewd glance noticed his flushed features, his loosened collar and tie and the fact that most of the buttons of his waistcoat were undone. After that one swift glance he busied himself with uncorking the fresh bottle.

M. Pinaud raised his glass and as the innkeeper bent down to pull the cork, he emptied its contents in one swift movement into the gap of his unbottoned waistcoat.

Then he sighed profoundly and sat there stoically with the wine seeping coldly and wetly through his shirt and around his belly, and watched the two glasses being re-filled with an expression of owlish concentration.

"Sit down and have it with me," M. Pinaud enunciated carefully. "Man was not made to drink alone."

"You are very generous, m'sieu," Dubois replied with punctilious courtesy. "I accept willingly, but only on the condition that you will permit me to offer you a bottle as my guest."

"That," declared M. Pinaud "is a very right and proper

speech. But I do not think I shall be able to accept. I have already had enough of this remarkable wine."

"Nonsense," replied the innkeeper. "No one could ever have too much of a wine like this."

"Maybe—maybe," agreed M. Pinaud. "After all—it is the wine of the Popes."

He lifted his glass and sipped a little slowly.

"Wonderful."

Then he yawned gigantically.

"I shall soon be ready for bed," he muttered. Then he began slapping his pockets.

"Now—curse it—where did I leave them? It must have been in the bedroom——"

"What is that, m'sieu?"

"My cigarettes. I left them upstairs——"

"I will go."

"No—no—I should have remembered."

"Please do not move. I will get them for you."

"You are extremely kind. The packet must be on the bed or the dressing-table."

Dubois stood up. As soon as his back was turned, M. Pinaud emptied his glass in the same place and when the innkeeper turned round at the door he was already reaching for the bottle.

Again, as soon as he was alone, M. Pinaud poured half the bottle into the other urn, and as he sprawled in his chair waiting for the man to come back he reflected that this was truly the most noble wine he had ever tasted. But he had no thought of regret at having wasted it. In the accomplishment of his duty M. Pinaud was completely single-minded.

The innkeeper came back into the room. M. Pinaud

ignored him. He stared at the tablecloth with a determined intensity.

The innkeeper glanced at him and then at the bottle on the table.

"M'sieu Pinaud," he said quietly, "I am going to fetch another bottle. Would you care to accompany me?"

"What's that—oh yes—delighted."

And M. Pinaud, not without difficulty, heaved himself up to his feet.

"The cellars here are most interesting," continued the innkeeper. "They extend as far as the church of Notre Dame and they are even older than this building, which dates from the fifteenth century."

"Really?"

M. Pinaud followed the man down a passage, staggering a little as he walked.

Dubois stopped in front of a door, and taking a huge key from his pocket, he fitted it into the lock. Pushing the door open, he stood aside politely.

M. Pinaud walked into another small room, whose floor was of uneven stone cobbles. In the centre of this room was a rectangular opening with a flight of wooden steps leading down into the cellars. The innkeeper touched a switch on the wall and M. Pinaud could see the stone floor illuminated below.

Without hesitation he lurched towards the opening.

"Hadn't you better go first?" he asked, without pausing. "After all—it is your cellar. You know the way better than I do."

The innkeeper laughed.

"It is quite easy—straight down the steps."

"Very well."

M. Pinaud had taken two steps down when he felt a violent push in his back.

With all his senses alert he had been expecting something of this kind, and therefore his reaction was quick enough to be effective. He bent at the knees to bring his body lower and flung himself sideways with desperate quickness. His outstretched hand caught one of the steps and for a second he clung there until his other hand found a hold.

Then he felt a sudden swift stab of agony on his fingers, and the pain spurred him on to a great effort. With one gigantic heave he pulled himself up by bending his arms, let go with one hand, and grasping the innkeeper's ankle with the other, jerked with all his strength.

There was a wild yell as the man lost his balance and then an indescribable and horrifying sound as he hit the stone floor.

M. Pinaud hauled himself back on the steps and sat there for a little while until he had stopped trembling.

Again M. Pinaud sat on the bed. Again M. Pinaud smoked and thought. And again he liberally besprinkled the bedclothes with the ash that dropped unheeded from his waistcoat and his trousers.

But this time he had removed his boots and his thoughts were no longer vague and confused; now they were clear and keen and cold with that incisive and brilliant clarity which had penetrated so many obscure and baffling problems to the credit of the *Sûreté*, the renown of M. le Chef and—let it be admitted—to the eternal honour and glory of M. Pinaud.

The case was warming up. Someone did not like him investigating. Someone did not like him staying in

Chassagne. Someone—since that pitiful body in the cellar could be nothing more than a tool—wished to be left in peace to perpetuate whatever warped satisfaction they derived in severing heads from bodies. Someone did not wish to be disturbed.

It had not been a bad idea.

M. Pinaud, whose fondness for good wine and food was well known, had discovered and sampled that exquisite vintage, of whose existence and potency a dozen witnesses could probably testify. M. Pinaud, who although an individualist yet nevertheless remained a democrat, had invited the inkeeper to drink with him, since drinking is not a pastime in which the wise man indulges alone. Stimulated by the company, M. Pinaud had drunk perhaps a little more than he should. Unaccustomed to wine of such quality—since it was notorious that the salaries of the *Sûreté* had never been commensurate with the labours they involved—M. Pinaud had perhaps made the completely understandable error of misjudging and underestimating the potentialities of its effects. Overwhelmed by the flavour of its taste, what more natural than that M. Pinaud should venture to descend into the cellar to fetch another bottle?

"I told him to take care," the innkeeper would have mouthed unctuously, striving to keep his shifty regard on the *Juge d' Instruction*. "I warned him that the steps were steep."

"How lamentable—what a tragedy!" all the witnesses would exclaim in pious horror. "A promising career, cut off in its prime. But Mercurey is a strong wine—a most potent wine. It is the wine of the Popes—and they ought to know."

M. Pinaud grinned sardonically.

And then the *Juge d' Instruction* would have returned a verdict of death by misadventure and added a rider and a recommendation in his report to the *Sûreté*—for whom he no doubt entertained a fitting legal contempt—that either the salaries of their operatives be increased to enable them to live and carry their liquor like gentlemen, or alternatively, that special wine-tasting classes be added to their curriculum of fingerprint smudging, bloodhound following, keyhole snooping and witness beating in order that perhaps the unfortunate death of this citiden Pinaud might be utilized as an example from which future and similar pitfalls might be avoided. . . . It would no doubt have been an impressive document.

M. Pinaud lit another cigarette. It was late and he was tired, but he had no desire to go to sleep. The plot had failed and he was still alive. It was not the first time that the removal and the elimination of Pinaud had been tried, and it would surely not be the last.

Someone—but who?

A corpse with a cracked skull was hardly likely to that perhaps the unfortunate death of this citizen Pinaud realized that he was no nearer the solution than he had been before.

For a moment he felt compunction—that sorrow which never failed to accompany the emotion in his cases, either as a sudden stab or a slow, silent stealing, a sorrow that stayed with him, softly and sadly, long after the case was closed. He was a humane man and a compassionate one; in his work these qualities were tested to the utmost limit of endurance. It is to his credit that he emerged from the ordeal his work made of his life with these qualities untouched, unaffected and unchanged. If anything, they were strengthened and intensified by all the violence and misery and bloodshed he was compelled to witness and endure.

For a moment he felt compunction and pity. A man's life, however unworthy, however misused, had ended—and all the cold tragic finality of that irrevocable ending seemed suddenly to rise up and overwhelm him, since he had been the cause of that ending. For a moment he bowed his head, alone there in the quiet solemnity of the night. This was the worst part. This was the part that he hated. This was the part that always made his achievements seem like child's play, his triumphs a mockery and his success a folly.

But in his nature the realist and the idealist were nicely balanced. Mercifully, these moments did not last.

He raised his head after a while in a gesture of unconscious defiance, and lit another cigarette. It had been his life or the other's. The attack had been unprovoked, swift and savage and merciless. He had defended himself in the only way possible under the circumstances. That had resulted in the death of Dubois, but Dubois should have thought of that before he started.

The moment passed as suddenly and as swiftly as it had come. M. Pinaud resumed his thinking.

You take a corpse. Without a head. And, incredibly, without finger-tips. You find it—of all the impossible places—in a garden. Then you find another corpse, also without a head, on a railway line, where obviously it had been placed after death. Were these two corpses connected? Did one have anything to do with the other? In that case, had the second one been removed from the garden?

Were they both connected in some way with the old lady? And was there any truth in her accusations—would two normal and apparently sane people go to such lengths to satisfy a grudge? If that were not true, why had she made them? Why seek to implicate people in a crime that was apparently motiveless? Yet all crime had a motive. Only madmen killed without reason. Was that the reason—was Roland mad? Surely in that case they would have known—surely if he tended to violence they would never have kept him there—the hospital would never have discharged him or allowed him to go. When it does happen, she had said, I am with him. He is at home, surrounded by those who love him. We can look after him. Surely she could not have said that had he been violent. It sounded rather as if he became witless or vacant, as if his intelligence died beneath the weight of the horrors he remembered. . . .

There were other things, too, which seemed to surge chaotically through M. Pinaud's thoughts. There was this mysterious illness of Marie Capt. He must remember to ask Dr. Reuge for more details about that in the morning. He must also see M. le Commissaire in the morning and explain about the body of Dubois—there was also something else—something important . . .

At this juncture M. Pinaud's head fell back on the pillow and he fell fast asleep. His burning cigarette dropped from his limply relaxed fingers, but mercifully landed inside one of his square-toed boots where it soon gave up any attempt to ignite the perspiration-soaked leather and smouldered itself out into ash.

Chapter Five

THE next morning M. Pinaud finished his breakfast un-hurriedly and then rang the bell. When the plump young girl appeared he leaned back in his chair and lit a cigarette.

"Tell me," he said quietly, "did M'sieu Dubois have any family?"

She stared at him in astonishment.

"Not that I know of, m'sieu. He lived here alone."

"Good. Then that will make it easier. I am sorry to have to inform you that M'sieu Dubois met with an accident last night."

"An accident?"

"Yes. You might call it that. He fell down the cellar steps. Please do not go into the cellar, mademoiselle. I will arrange for the body to be taken away."

"Then he is dead?"

"Yes."

Two large tears welled up into the girl's eyes, brimmed over and coursed down her cheeks. M. Pinaud regarded her curiously, and when he spoke his voice was gentle.

"You—you were fond of him?"

"Oh no, m'sieu. But to be dead—that is awful."

M. Pinaud nodded gravely. Her grief was probably far more sincere: she did not weep for the man, but for the awful desolation of death.

"You are right, mademoiselle," he said quietly. "It is awful for those who remain. Whatever it is awful for those who experience it—that is something we shall never know. Meanwhile—if you would just continue for the time being with your duties, I will make all the necessary arrangements."

"Thank you, m'sieu."

M. Pinaud then made his way across the market-place to the *gendarmerie*. M. le Commissaire was not there. The policeman on duty informed him that M. Minoton had sent a message to say that he would be absent the whole day. No, he had not mentioned where he was going.

M. Pinaud sighed with frustration and drummed impatiently with his fingers on the desk.

"Tell me—where can I find M'sieu le Maire?"

"At the *Mairie*, m'sieu—the tall building with the carvings at the far end of the street."

"Thank you—oh, by the way—get the ambulance to the hotel as soon as possible. The body of Dubois the innkeeper is in the cellar. Get it taken to the morgue pending the inquest. Dr. Reuge can look at it, if he has a moment, but it is really a waste of time. Cause of death—broken neck or broken head. He fell down the steps."

And he went out, leaving the policeman gaping with open mouth.

The sun was shining. M. Pinaud walked slowly, seeing the town of Chassagne as if for the first time.

The day before he had driven his car over the same cobbles, but so much had occupied his mind that his memory retained nothing of what his eyes had seen. Now, as he walked, it was as if he saw it all for the first time.

The main road, cobbled and uneven, ran wide and straight through the uneven bulging of the medieval buildings. Steeply cambered each side, its centre was a gutter, along which water always flowed from the huge circular fountain outside the Town Hall. Some of the buildings had their upper floors supported on massive stone arches, forming arcades through which the narrow pavement ran. As if in contempt for the shadowed seclusion of these ground-floor windows, barrows and stalls displayed their wares in the sunshine on both sides of the street. With these and the lorries and cars which were parked beside them, the vast width of the road was reduced to two narrow lanes on either side of the gutter.

M. Pinaud kept to the pavement, passing from the cool velvet shadow of the arcades out into the clear vivid sunshine until he reached the exquisitely carved façades of the Town Hall.

M. le Maire was in his office, and M. le Maire was gracious enough to receive him without delay, and M. le Maire was polite enough to wave him into a comfortable chair; but to say that M. le Maire was pleased at what he had to relate would have been a statement of the wildest inexactitude.

"But this is terrible, M'sieu Pinaud! It is monstrous— it is unbelievable. . . ."

"Nevertheless, M'sieu le Marie, it is true," interrupted M. Pinaud calmly, fumbling in his pockets for his cigarettes.

M. le Marie, who had been spluttering in his agitation in a manner hardly befitting the dignity of his office, suddenly grew ominously calm.

"But there is no proof. You say you went down into the cellar together and you say that he tried to push you down, but failed, and you say you pushed him down instead?"

M. Pinaud's hands continued to fumble in his pockets, but suddenly his brain seemed to grow ice-cold and clear.

"That is correct, m'sieu," he replied quietly. "That is what I say."

His hand brought out a packet of cigarettes. He extracted one and lit it slowly and his hands were perfectly steady. His voice, too, was quite calm as he continued.

"There is no proof. It is a matter of accepting my word. Or had Dubois lived, it would have been his word against mine."

"But he is dead."

"Exactly. Therefore you will have to accept my word."

For a long moment their eyes met and held—M. le Maire's hotly angry and suspicious, M. Pinaud's cold and hard and implacable. It was M. le Maire who first looked down.

"I don't like it," he muttered. "The whole thing seems incredible. Why on earth should Dubois try to kill you? He has never seen you before—or has he? Did you know him?"

"I never set eyes on him until yesterday," replied M. Pinaud. "Your question, m'sieu, is quite logical, but beside the point. We are not dealing with Dubois, but with a murderer—the man responsible for the two headless corpses. The man who is not happy now that Pinaud is investigating. Dubois was obviously his tool. Either the murderer paid him or had some hold over him. Did Dubois make money out of his hotel?"

"No. It was left to him by his father. We are off the track of the tourists here, m'sieu—whole days pass without a guest in the hotel. Dubois spent most of his time sampling his father's cellar, which was an extensive one."

"When we search his room or his pockets we may find some money, which perhaps will help to convince you. And if not, then we shall have to wait until I have found the murderer. Until then, M'sieu le Maire, I can only ask you to accept my word and be patient."

And with that M. Pinaud stood up. M. le Maire stood up as well and began to mutter to himself. Suddenly he stopped muttering and began to swell visibly with his own importance.

"And what if I don't?"

"Then I shall telephone to Paris for a warrant and arrest you for obstructing justice," answered M. Pinaud quietly. "You may be a very important man in Chassagne, M'sieu le Maire, but let me remind you that your power is nothing compared to the authority vested in me by the State."

For a moment there was silence. M. Pinaud's words had been quiet, almost casual, but with them it was as if a dark curtain had been suddenly swept aside and a vivid blaze of light had illuminated the majestic solemnity of the power he represented.

M. le Maire sat down abruptly. Suddenly he seemed old and frail and very tired.

"I thought you were going to help us, M'sieu Pinaud," he said quietly and yet with great dignity. "I had the impression yesterday that you were the man to rid us of this horror—and now, the day after you arrive, we have yet another death . . .!

"I know. I am sorry," M. Pinaud interrupted with ready sympathy. "This business of Dubois is unfortunate—but I can assure you it was not of my seeking. It was my life or his. I had to defend myself. But do not worry. I will solve this mystery as I have solved others before. You need not worry—it is the murderer who is getting worried. He knows that Pinaud is on the trail and he does not like it. Just give me a little time, M'sieu le Maire, and all your worries will be over."

And with that M. Panaud bowed himself out.

M. le Chef was liverish and the line to Paris was bad. M. Pinaud maintained his equanimity with the utmost difficulty.

"But this is ridiculous," the wrathful voice crackled irascibly in his ear. "Mad and ridiculous. I am surprised at you, Pinaud. Here you find yourself with a couple of corpses on your hands with never a clue to help, and all you do is saddle yourself with a third. Are you quite sure he is dead?"

"He fell head first on a stone floor," replied M. Pinaud patiently. "I heard his skull crack."

"Why the devil couldn't you get a witness?"

M. Pinaud sighed. He could just imagine M. le Chef sitting at his huge desk, the telephone gripped fiercely and tightly in his hand and clamped hard against his ear, his complexion slowly turning from red to magenta and from magenta to puce as his blood pressure surged inexorably higher in sympathy with the mounting tension of his nerves.

It would be so much easier for everyone if he remained calm. It was not difficult to remain calm—at least, not too difficult. Other people had had to learn how to do it, in the face of complexities and problems which M. le Chef could not possibly imagine—which indeed would bring him to a speedy end with a merciful stroke were he ever to be confronted with them. Other people, in subordinate positions, were compelled to learn this difficult lesson—why not M. le Chef?

Then he took a deep breath and spoke with measured calm.

"When a man is trying to commit murder he usually

arranges to be alone with his intended victim. No one was invited."

"I know—I know. But couldn't you have found some-one? Surely you could have awoken some other guest."

"There are no other guests. I was alone in the hotel. The maid comes every morning. Did you want me to go out in the town and drag some respectable citizen from his bed and invite him to come and look at the corpse of Dubois and verify that he had met an end which was both violent and just? What could he witness? That the man was dead?"

"There is no need to be sarcastic, Pinaud. I don't like this. I don't like it at all. You may have trouble with the locals. What does the Commissaire say?"

"Well," admitted M. Pinaud reluctantly, "he seems to be away today, following up some clue."

M. le Chef groaned. M. Pinaud hastened to continue.

"But I have already reported it to the Mayor. There is no need to worry on that account."

"I still say I don't like it, Pinaud. I tell you what—I'll send you another man right away."

"But I don't want another man, m'sieu. I am perfectly capable——"

"I know you are capable, Pinaud. Everyone knows you are competent and capable. This is no reflection on your skill or your ability. But you understand—it may be a question of the wood and the trees. A fresh opinion—a new viewpoint—another outlook . ."

M. Pinaud sighed. It was difficult not to feel resentment. But he knew it was no use arguing with M. le Chef in this mood. It had been a mistake to try sarcasm.

"Very well, m'sieu."

"His name is Charles Valin. A most promising youngster—keen and capable and related to the Minister himself. It will do him a world of good to work with you and I am sure he will be of use. I'll send him off at once. Let me know how you get on. Good-bye."

M. Pinaud sighed again as he replaced the receiver. It was an unjust world. Great a man might be, and yet so unfairly was it constituted that there was always a greater to whom he had to submit.

Keen and capable indeed. His sigh became a snort of pure disgust. Related to the Minister—pah! One of these young bounders who would poke their confounded noses into everything and everyone's business for two years and then automatically assume positions of executive importance, having had practical experience, look you, and worked their way up, mark you, from the very bottom of the ladder. . . .

M. Pinaud remembered just in time that he was in the office of M. le Commissaire, which although adequately furnished in every other respect, yet did not cater for the needs of those whose disgust assumed proportions violent enough to be assuaged only by an expression of contempt drastic and emphatic and physical. . . .

Instead he lit a cigarette and began to make copious notes in his notebook.

In the afternoon Charles Valin arrived.

M. Pinaud looked out from the window and snorted in disgust at the sight of the lavender and pink sports car. When its owner emerged he regretted that he had wasted his snort on the car. Charles Valin, in a suit of immaculate cut, whose shade matched perfectly one half of the car's colour scheme, and a shirt and tie which toned admirably with the other—Charles Valin, small and

72

slender and sleek and faultlessly groomed, was all that he had feared and more.

Sighing philosophically, he left the window and went to meet him, his features impassive, his hand outstretched in greeting.

"M'sieu Valin? I am Pinaud. Welcome to Chassagne."

The young exquisite offered a hand like a piece of wet fish.

"What a one-eyed dump. The sooner I get out of here the better."

M. Pinaud decided to ignore this.

"If you will come into the office," he said equably, "I will put you in the picture."

Whatever his feelings, M. Pinaud was scrupulously fair. He sat down at M. Minoton's desk and recounted, clearly and dispassionately, the substance of what had happened since he set out with the wife of M. le Chef.

Charles Valin listened attentively enough, but made no attempt to conceal his boredom. When M. Pinaud had finished he politely stifled a yawn behind two delicately manicured fingers.

"I should have thought it obvious, M'sieu Pinaud," he remarked coolly. "Rostand the butcher—there's your man."

M. Pinaud stared. Self-confidence was a good thing, especially in the young. But this complacency—this arrogance—this was something he could not understand. He remembered his own youth and his own humble beginnings, when he had taken those first steps which were to lead him so far along the path of fame, when all the world and M. le Chef had been against him, when nothing had upheld him save his own passionate conviction that he was right and everyone else was wrong—but that had been self-confidence. That had been something different. Events and the acclaim of millions had proved how different.

But for this upstart—this nobody—to voice such an opinion with such insufferable arrogance immediately after hearing the facts of the case, when hours of mature and considered reflection by the brain of the greatest detective in France had produced nothing more than a bewildering mass of contradictions—this was really too much.

In the past M. Pinaud's opinion may have differed from the accepted decisions of the majority, but even if it had he always retained the good sense to keep it to himself until he could substantiate it with logical and unanswerable proof and, moreover, the good manners to refrain from airing it in the presence of his superiors.

There was no doubt about it. The world was changing, and not for the better.

But none of these thoughts, nothing of these reflections showed on his impassive countenance as he lit another cigarette and answered the young detective lolling negligently opposite him.

"You think so?"

After all, this—this visitation—this burden had been laid upon him by M. le Chef himself, and M. le Chef, whatever his faults and his limitations, whatever his shortcomings and his deficiencies, was nevertheless responsible for M. Pinaud's salary, and M. Pinaud's salary was the foundation on which rested the happiness and the peace of mind of his wife and the welfare of his children. Therefore M. le Chef was something, in M. Pinaud's philosophy, which one accepted without arguing, even though positive in one's mind that his place could easily and certainly be filled by several, and notably one, of the employees over whom he took such delight in playing God.

"I do think so—definitely. It all points to him. I will go myself and ask this Rostand some questions—questions which he will find difficult to answer."

M. Pinaud did not reply. M. Pinaud just looked at him.

"That is, of course," the young man hastily added, in a somewhat more diffident tone, "if you have no objection?"

Still M. Pinaud continued to look at him. Then, suddenly, he roused himself.

"Objection—oh yes—I mean no—no. None at all. You go ahead. You do as you think fit. I will see you again when you come back. His shop is about halfway down the main road, on the right-hand side."

When Charles Valin had gone without a word of thanks, M. Pinaud continued to sit at the desk for a long time, lost in thought.

His eyes gazed out through the window at the serene blue vault of the tranquil sky, and they remained fixed in absorption, but gradually and slowly the grimness of his features relaxed into an impish grin. Charles Valin questioning Rostand the butcher. This should be funny.

It was funny. Even funnier than he had anticipated. And in an entirely unexpected way.

After about fifteen minutes M. Pinaud decided to visit M. Minoton's landlady, in the hope that she might have some clue as to where the Commissaire had gone.

He left the office and walked down the main road towards the address he had found on a file.

As he approached the shop of Rostand the butcher, his attention was suddenly caught by an extraordinary sight.

The door was opened with a violence that almost tore it off its hinges. The figure of Charles Valin was ejected,

forcibly and violently, from the inside of the shop. Then
the door was slammed, so hard that it seemed as if the
ancient building rocked on its foundations.

The figure Charles Valin presented was somewhat
different from his usual immaculate self. His collar and
tie had been wrenched completely off and the beautiful
suit was crumpled and torn and stained hideously with
blood. Pieces of suet and sausage-meat were all over him,
even in his hair.

M. Pinaud wondered if he had been hurt, but the
spectacle of the infuriated young man, who was literally
dancing with rage, brought to his mind the various cuts
of bloodstained meat which were normally to be found
within the shop of Rostand the butcher, and he realized
what must have happened.

For a moment Charles Valin continued to dance. Then
he hurled himself at the door, beating at its stout panels
with his fists and kicking it with a fury which unfortunately had more effect on his beautiful shoes than on the
weatherbeaten and toughened oak of the door.

"Open—open this door!" he yelled. "Open in the name
of the law!"

But the door did not open.

Charles Valin then turned his attention to the window,
but the massive plate-glass had been fired and blown three
hundred years ago and its strength and solidity defied
even the fury of that impassioned attack, as it would
have defied the onslaught of anything less than a sledge-
hammer.

Charles Valin soon realized this and returned with
renewed fury to the door.

M. Pinaud, whom amazement had literally rooted to
the pavement, was about to hurry forward to stop him

when he felt a hand on his arm. He turned. It was M. le Maire.

"And what, may I ask," demanded M. le Maire heavily, "is the meaning of this—this insensate outrage to our standards of public behaviour?"

"Why ask me?" retorted M. Pinaud coolly.

M. le Maire made a great effort to keep calm.

"I ask you, M'sieu Pinaud, for two very good reasons. One is that I do not recognize that young man's face— and I flatter myself that I know every face in Chassagne. Therefore he is a stranger here—the second stranger here. You are the first. It is logical to assume that there may be a connection.

"The other reason is that since you appeared on the scene we appear to have nothing but trouble in this town. I can assure you I have never witnessed such a disgraceful and malicious exhibition of temper in this street in all my years of office. Therefore again I maintain it's only logical to assume that this is but a further manifestation of the calamity which has stricken our town and to presume that —as for everything else—you are the one responsible."

"Your reasoning is magnificent," M. Pinaud told him, "but only half right. His name is Charles Valin and he has been sent by the *Sûreté* to assist me in this case. Apart from that I know nothing. Let us find out what has happened."

It did not take them long to reach Charles Valin, but quite long enough to hear some of the comments from the crowd that was rapidly growing around the infuriated young man.

"It is another one with whom Rostand has quarrelled. . . . "

"No—it is for a bet."

77

"Perhaps for the new film *sonore*. . . . "

'He said in the name of the law—he looks more like a species of gangster to me."

"But why should he rub himself in suet before attacking the door?"

"Wrestlers oil their bodies . . ."

"But this is suet . . ."

"And sausage-meat."

"That was the quarrel—the price of the suet . . ."

"But the shop is closed . . ."

"Rostand must be dead. This one is bleeding . . ."

All this and much more M. Pinaud heard before M. le Maire finally planted himself fairly and squarely in front of the *protégé* of M. le Chef.

"What do you think you are doing, behaving like this in the main road of Chassagne? Is it a vendetta—a blood feud? Are you a Corsican?"

Charles Valin was not very far from tears—tears of vexation and humiliation and frustration, but he took one glance at M. Pinaud and answered patiently enough.

"No. It is not a vendetta. Neither am I a Corsican."

"I am glad to hear it. Then there will be no problem of extradiction," retorted M. le Maire belligerently.

"What do you mean?"

"What I say. I am going to charge you with disorderly conduct in a public thoroughfare and lock you up in a cell. If you think you can come to Chassagne and behave in this outrageous manner——"

"Now wait a moment," interrupted M. Pinaud suddenly. Taking advantage of the sudden amazed hush, since when M. le Maire was speaking it was unheard of to interrupt, he turned to Charles Valin.

"How did this happen?" he asked.

"It was Rostand. We had words—and then there was an argument amongst the meat."

"Right," said M. Pinaud. Then he turned to M. le Maire.

"I think it would be better, M'sieu le Maire," he suggested gently, "if we drop all this talk of charging and prison cells and agree to forget the whole thing, don't you? Because if you persist in charging M'sieu Valin I shall have no alternative but to bring a countercharge against M'sieu Rostand for assault, and for every moment that M'sieu Valin spends in a cell the amount of damages we shall claim will increase by fifty per cent, and if M'sieu Rostand should find himself ruined as a result of the case and if he should learn who was really responsible by insisting on this charge, then he might prove to be a bad enemy, don't you agree? He is a powerful man, and a violent one, and if he turned vindictive I should think he might easily prove to be a dangerous one."

And without waiting for an answer M. Pinaud took Charles Valin by the arm and guided him back to the *gendarmerie*, leaving M. le Maire open-mouthed on the pavement.

"Come," he said gently. "When all this crowd has gone you will have to see about some clothes."

He did not smile. There was no triumph in his voice, only an understanding and a compassion that warmed Charles Valin's heart.

After all, the young have to learn through bitter experience. And learning is hard enough without making it more difficult by saying I told you so.

M. Minoton's landlady was excessively polite to a member of the *Sûreté* as could be expected from one who had the privilege of cooking meals and darning socks for M. le Commissaire, but quite unable to help.

M. Minoton never confided business matters to anyone —oh, no—and quite right too, in his opinion—implying that M. Pinaud ought to know better than to ask—there were reasons of security involved in all matters of an official nature and therefore nothing was discussed outside his office.

M. Pinaud thanked her politely and retraced his steps. It had been a forlorn hope. It looked as though M. Minoton was on the trail of something; it would be a good thing when he returned.

At the *gendarmerie* he was just in time to see Charles Valin, comparatively clean but still clad in the ruin of his suit, about to climb into his beautiful sports car.

"Hullo," he said. "Where are you going?"

"Back to Paris, M'sieu Pinaud—with your permission," replied a very subdued Charles Valin, "to get some clothes."

"Why not buy some here?"

Charles Valin stared in honest bewilderment.

"I could not do that."

"Why not?"

"I could not wear a ready-made suit. If you don't mind, m'sieu, I would sooner get one of my own."

"As you wish."

"I will be back in the morning. Is there anything special you would like me to do?"

M. Pinaud considered gravely. It would appear that in this case the seed had fallen on fertile ground.

"Not really. I will have to go to the Château again tomorrow, but I don't think there is any point in two of us being there. We must see M'sieu Minoton as soon as he appears; he may have work for us as a result of his investigations. If not, the only thing to do is to check again on Jean Falange's acquaintances and see if you can pick up a clue. The list should be somewhere on the file—you can take it in the morning."

"Very good, m'sieu. And——"

He started to say something else and then changed his mind. Quickly he climbed into the car and drove off.

M. Pinaud watched him go thoughtfully. There was good material here, in spite of his being related to the Minister. In a few more years, if he absorbed all of life's lessons as readily as he had the bitterness of this one, he would be well on the way to becoming a detective. After that, a few more years of failure and frustration and acquiring knowledge and experience and he would have his feet firmly planted on the path that led to becoming a first-class detective. After that, it was up to him. Who could tell? If he really persevered, he might even in the fullness of time come to emulate the greatest of them all!

He wondered what colour the new suit would be. He must remember to speak to Rostand about that in the morning. He hoped Valin would take the hint and not come poking his nose into the Château. There was enough trouble and difficulty in that household without adding to it.

He must also remember to see M. Minoton first thing in the morning and explain about the business of Dubois and settle all the formalities in the proper manner.

Chapter Six

IN the morning there was no difficulty in seeing M. le Commissaire. The difficulty, however, would have arisen in attempting to explain anything to him, since the head of M. Minoton, neatly severed, lay several metres from the body of M. Minoton.

M. Pinaud stood in the garden of the Château, looking down with an impassive countenance which betrayed nothing of his true feelings.

This was the same as before. This followed the now expected pattern—even the finger-tips were there, laid neatly beside the body. And yet on the features of M. Minoton, indelibly stamped even in death, was such an expression of horror that M. Pinaud felt a slow and furious anger surging through his veins with the pulsing of his blood.

For a long time he stood there, bareheaded in the tranquil and mellow autumn sunshine. This harassed and kindly man had only been trying to do his duty. Slowly, and yet with a smooth and sweeping finality, as if a cloud had swept soundlessly across the sun, a cold and tragic sadness seemed to smother him in its embrace.

This was the end of all human endeavour; this was the goal to which all his triumphs and all his successes were leading him, inevitably, relentlessly, unmistakably. It might come to him in this way; it might be in another, but sooner or later he, too, would have to face it. The thought was somehow majestic in its solemnity and irrevocability, and yet at the same time poignant and wistful in a way which lessened its grandeur to the proportions of human understanding.

One day he would no longer take part; he would no longer be here, and yet the world would go on in exactly the same way—in the same way that everything was now continuing in spite of the headless body of M. Minoton, which lay there quietly at his feet, heedless and unknowing, insensitive and uncaring. The mystery remained unsolved, the murderer still walked free. Another victim had been added to the death-roll and M. Pinaud's task grew more difficult, but all this was happening without M. Minoton, since he was dead.

One day M. Pinaud, too, would be dead. Who would remember him? Who would mourn him—and for how long? Time has a savage way of obliterating even the most resounding of human triumphs and of dulling the edge of the most poignant sorrow. Time would pass and even M. Pinaud would be forgotten. It was a sobering thought and an almost terrifying one. M. Pinaud knew that there was no advantage to be gained in dwelling on it.

He welcomed the sudden swift surge of pity which came to replace and supplant it.

He felt pity for M. Minoton. He felt pity for all his kind—for the weak and the timid and the ineffectual—for the insecure and the hesitant and the bewildered. He felt a pity that was innocent of contempt, but blessed in that it would share of its strength—which was his strength—and help those who needed aid. He felt pity for all those who found the struggle too hard, for those whom life was continually beating, for those—like M. Minoton—who had paid, unjustly, to the full.

And even in his compassion he realized that this was the time when he needed his strength more than ever

He needed it for his own sake. And he needed it for the benefit of those who did not possess it. And he needed it so that he could triumph in his duty and avenge M. Minoton.

Then, rousing himself, he turned to the *gendarme* who stood respectfully behind him.

"What is your name?" he asked quietly.

"Bernard, m'sieu. Jules Bernard."

"Well, Bernard, this is a bad thing. Tell me: do you know anything that would help us in some way?"

"I don't think so, m'sieu."

"When did you see him last?"

"Yesterday—that is, last night. I was on duty and he looked in to say he was going out. Oh yes—and he said he would telephone if he needed me."

"Did he say where he was going?"

"No, m'sieu."

"Did he seem strange—different in any way?"

"Well, yes. He seemed excited; I remember wondering what was the matter, but as he did not say anything——"

"Yes—quite—he would not tell anyone. He said he had an idea—but he would not tell me what it was. Then, later, he said he wanted to verify his suspicions. . . . That is the danger of working alone—one has to be very good and very quick and very clever. . . ."

His voice ceased as again he looked down at the corpse for a moment. Then he sighed and turned his back on it.

"He must have found a clue. It is a pity he would not share it. He verified his suspicions all right—but he is hardly in a position to draw any conclusions from them. Who found the body?"

"The housekeeper here. Victoire. She telephoned us. I

was just going off duty, but I sent for you and came straight over here."

"Quite right. Well, if you have been on duty all night, the best thing you can do is to get some sleep. I will take over here. Have you sent for Dr. Reuge?"

"Yes, I telephoned. Here is his car now."

"Good. Off you go. I'll see you at the *gendarmerie* this afternoon."

"Thank you, m'sieu."

The enormous bonnet of the Bugatti swept up the drive and the huge car rocked on its springs as the hand-brake was savagely applied.

M. Pinaud returned to contemplate the body with a strange and almost intense absorption. Some remote cell at the back of his brain seemed to be trying to warm him, to send him a message which was in some way connected with the impression on his retina, but so many conscious thoughts were occupying his mind that the message could not penetrate.

Later, when he was quiet and relaxed and his sub-conscious mind open and receptive, he would realize and understand; now he was conscious of nothing more than a vague disquiet and unease, a consciousness and an awareness of something wrong, something that needed investigation, something he had to pursue. . . .

The doctor's expression was sombre as he hurried over to where M. Pinaud stood.

"Not another one—surely."

The resonant voice was fittingly muted, and yet even beneath the quiet words the power seemed to quiver as if eager to break free.

M. Pinaud gestured down towards the earth.

"Exactly the same," he replied briefly. "Would you examine it now and tell me what you think."

"Of course."

The doctor knelt and opened his bag. M. Pinaud turned away, feeling a little sick.

Here not only was the body of M. Minoton strangely, poignantly out of place beside these age-old stones and this tranquil walled garden, but now the examination seemed a desecration, the disturbance of a peace which the calm and the benediction of centuries had tried vainly and yet bravely to enshroud and enfold over all this alien violence.

And yet it had to be done. If there was anything to be learnt, it was his duty to learn it.

At length Dr. Reuge stood up, wiping his hands on a silk handkerchief.

"Just the same, M'sieu Pinaud."

"In every respect?"

"As far as I can see at the moment."

"Not enough blood?"

"No. It has been moved."

"The incision—the same weapon?"

"Obviously."

"The finger-tips?"

"Identical."

"I see."

The rapid violence of M. Pinaud's questions died as suddenly as it had begun. For a moment he stood there, frowning in thought. Then he spoke slowly and hesitantly, as if he were voicing his thoughts aloud.

"If you do not mind, M'sieu le Docteur, I would feel happier if I got another opinion from Paris."

"Of course."

"This is no reflection on your skill or your capabilities, but you understand—you have examined three of them—subconsciously you may be identifying characteristics of each. It may be a question of the wood and the trees—perhaps a fresh opinion—a new mind . . ." M. Pinaud derived a certain sardonic satisfaction from repeating the words of M. le Chef.

"I quite agree with you, m'sieu," replied the doctor easily. "Actually, I was going to suggest much the same thing myself. I do not mind confessing that I am absolutely bewildered, and I do not seem to be able to reach any definite or conclusive opinion which would be of help. A fresh unbiased diagnosis is what we need. Do you wish me to perform the autopsy?"

"Yes, by all means. Finish the thing completely and let me have your report. Then we will try to get some new ideas."

He lit a cigarette and walked back to the car with the doctor.

"Now we have had your professional report," he said, "let me have your private opinion as an individual. What do you think of all this?"

Dr. Reuge laughed shortly.

"My opinion?" I have none. I am baffled."

"By the method of the killing?"

The doctor stared.

"Of course—what else?"

"You misunderstand me. Let us leave the method on one side. Who do you think is responsible for these crimes?"

For a moment there was a silence, a stillness into which M. Pinaud's words seemed to have been engulfed and obliterated, and yet in whose vastness they still seemed to hover, unsaid and yet remembered, fearful in their significance.

Dr. Reuge stared out at nothing, his body completely still. Then he seemed to rouse himself and reach a decision. The brown eyes met and held those of M. Pinaud for a long moment as if seeking reassurance before he spoke. What he saw there seemed to satisfy him. He cleared his throat and his voice once again vibrated with all its habitual power.

"There is only one person it could be."

"I was afraid you would say that," replied M. Pinaud heavily.

"Afraid—why?"

"Because it will break the old lady's heart."

"Very probably, but what is the alternative?"

M. Pinaud sighed and looked down at the ground and then back to where the body of M. Minoton lay so strangely and so pitifully on the soft rich earth.

"More of this, probably. There is no alternative. What makes you so certain?"

"I am not certain. Please do not misunderstand me. There is nothing certain in this nightmare. I said there is only one person it could be—but that assumption is based on supposition."

"What supposition?"

"The negative one, in the first place, that there is no one else here who would do such a thing. The positive ones that he is not normal, that he is subject to fits of melancholia and hysteria, and that his overwhelming recollection of the war in the shocking experience——"

"I know, I know," interrupted M. Pinaud with a completely irrational irritation. "He told me about that."

"You must admit that the parallel is striking."

"I do."

"And that to kill in this senseless way—without reason or motive—is the work of a madman."

"About the first two I cannot say. But M. Minoton was killed because he had found out something."

"Indeed?"

"Yes. He told me yesterday that he had his suspicions, but he would not confide in me."

"That is a pity. Now it is too late."

"Yes."

M. Pinaud stood for a moment, frowning at his boots. When he spoke his voice was slow and hesitant.

"Everything you have said is true. It all fits in and seems to indicate a certain conclusion. And yet—and yet . . ."

"And yet what, m'sieu?"

M. Pinaud's eyes, shrewd and compelling, met those of the doctor squarely, and as he answered his voice rang with all its accustomed conviction.

"And yet I am not satisfied. I have spoken to him myself. Here is a man who is ill and proud—bitter and frustrated—trying to escape from the overwhelming terror of memories he finds too horrible to bear—but not a senseless maniac."

"No one has seen him in his bad periods—even I have been excluded. No one, except Madame Capt, knows what he is like or what he does."

"Surrounded by those who love him," murmured M. Pinaud softly.

"What did you say, m'sieu?"

"Nothing. I was thinking aloud. I was thinking what an amazing woman she must be to have assumed that responsibility. But I am still not satisfied. I must investigate further. I will have a word with Madame Capt to begin with. I need not detain you any longer, m'sieu. Oh yes—one more question—this illness of Mademoiselle Capt. . . ."

The doctor paused with his hand on the door of his car.

"That is a question, M'sieu Pinaud, which I am honestly and truthfully unable to answer. I and my colleagues can find nothing organically unsound—and yet there is something wrong. Personally, I am inclined to think that it is something in the nature of an anxiety neurosis—and if you ask my opinion, the root of that anxiety lies in what we have just been discussing."

"Are you treating her?"

"A harmless sedative—hoping that it will have a psychological effect. There is no treatment—as long as she remains in this house."

"I see. I think you are right. Well, I will arrange for Dr. Vinet to come from Paris as soon as he is free. It may take a day or two, as he is a busy man."

"All right," replied Dr. Reuge as he climbed into his car. "I will let you have a report as soon as I have finished."

And in a shower of gravel the huge car shot off down the drive.

Once again M. Pinaud faced Madame Capt in the silence of her luxurious, old-fashioned room.

The old lady's features were lined and ravaged with fatigue and pain, and yet she held her head as proudly as ever and nothing could dim the fire in her sunken and shadowed eyes. So she would hold her head, M. Pinaud thought, even when she felt the Angel of Death beside her; so she would walk to meet the unknown, with a pride that transcended all fear.

"You wished to see me, M'sieu Pinaud?"

"Yes, madame," replied M. Pinaud gently. "I am afraid that I must trouble you once again with questions regarding your son Roland. Is he in?"

The blood drained from her face as she stared at him, leaving it an ashen mask out of whose pallor her eyes seemed to glow, the only living things in a cast of death.

"No, he has gone to town."

"Well, it is not urgent. I can see him when he returns."

"No—no. I know what you are thinking. It is not true. Believe me, m'sieu—it is not true."

M. Pinaud found it difficult to retain his composure before that extraordinary and heart-rending vehemence.

"What do you mean, madame? I have not said anything."

"There is no need. I know what you are thinking. This new horror this morning—the body of M'sieu Minoton. I know what you want to do. I have known it all along. You are going to accuse my son Roland."

"It has not yet reached a state of accusation, madame," replied M. Pinaud. "I merely wish to question him."

Suddenly, amazingly, the shadow of a smile came to soften the harsh lines of that suffering face; suddenly, poignantly, M. Pinaud had a glimpse of the beauty that once must have been hers. For a moment he was reminded of her daughter; in Marie that same loveliness seemed to sleep, in the old lady's features it had died, but her smile resurrected it and brought it, wonderfully, vitally alive.

"You are kind, M'sieu Pinaud," she said. "You are kind with a compassion which is merciful. The good God will surely bless you for such kindness. But keep it for those who are worthy. Do not waste it on me. I have suffered to a point when I no longer need kindness. And yet because of your kindness I would not have you make such a tragic mistake."

Suddenly she forced herself up out of the chair and came to stand before him.

"Listen, M'sieu Pinaud. Last night I could not sleep—it often happens with the pain in my ear. I am used to it, I do not complain. I snatch a few hours' rest in the day and make up for what I have lost. But last night—I swear to you—I did not sleep. I walked about this house, for hour after hour, alone with my pain and my memories.

"There is so much to remember in this house, m'sieu—here my ancestors were born and lived and made history and died—all beneath this roof above us. Here in this house their spirits walk with whoever walks at night, and so one is never really alone.

"But do you know what I did, m'sieu—I can see that you have enough imagination to answer my question yourself. I went into their bedrooms—not once but many times—and watched them as they lay sleeping, with their heads tranquil on their pillows and the moonlight streaming in the windows.

"I watched them and thought about them—my son and my daughter—and I remember the days when the beds were cots and I remembered that yesterday when they were children and small and helpless and dependent. Only a foolish old woman, you will say, m'sieu—dreaming and seeking refuge in the make-believe with which every mother seeks to hide the tragedy of reality—that children grow up and become other persons and need no help and no comfort and no love. That may be—and yet I was up and I watched them—throughout the night I was in and out of his room. How could he have got up without my knowing it? How could he have done anything like that?"

"You would swear to this, madame?"

"Of course I would swear to it. I have spoken the truth."

"And last night—you were in the garden?"

"We walked there, at dusk. Everything was—was as it should have been."

"And this morning?"

"I was already up, as I told you. Victoire came running to tell me at six o'clock. She saw—she saw it from her window when she got up."

"And what did you do?"

"I went straight to their bedrooms. They were both sound asleep. I did not disturb them. I left them and telephoned to the police."

"And did you hear anything in the night?"

"In a house like this, m'sieu, one always hears things. There are beams which contract with the pressure of centuries—there is mortar which crumbles and stones which sink with the weight of ages. A house such as this is always alive—especially in the dead of night. Of course I heard noises, but I took no notice. They were only the background to my memories."

M. Pinaud sighed. All this might be true, but it was not helping his investigations.

"One last thing, madame," he said gently. "What you told me last time I spoke to you—when your son Roland was bad you looked after him—what did you mean by bad?"

For a long moment she looked at him. Perhaps the compassion and the understanding in his eyes gave her the strength to speak.

"He becomes like a new-born child. His muscles have no strength, his nerves have no responses. His mind is completely vacant, he cannot speak; I do not think he can see. He—shall I go on?"

M. Pinaud shook his head. Then he reached out and laid his hands, gently and with infinite tenderness, on her shoulders.

"Courage, madame," he said. "Remember that he was a soldier of France."

Chapter Seven

ROSTAND the butcher eyed M. Pinaud with a malignant scowl. On a person of his proportions a scowl assumed terrifying capabilities, but M. Pinaud was not intimidated. He sat at M. le Commissaire's desk and listened calmly.

"I know I am suspect. You yourself have already told me that I am suspect—only because you are not capable of apprehendng the murderer. But is that any excuse for making me close my shop and waste the afternoon up here? How do you think I am going to earn my living? I have a good mind to pick up this desk and flatten you behind it."

And his huge hands opened and closed convulsively as if eager to put the threat into action.

M. Pinaud lit a cigarette calmly.

"You are welcome to try," he stated without emotion. "Whatever the outcome, and whatever the ancillary results, you will have to pay for a new one. And while you are on the subject of closing your shop and making such a fuss about earning your living, I do not seem to recall that these scruples—so commendable in themselves —were active enough to hinder you from doing exactly the same thing yesterday afternoon."

Most of Rostand's belligerency collapsed, as suddenly as a pricked balloon.

"Oh—that . . ." he muttered.

"Yes. That. The matter of M'sieu Charles Valin, detective, of the *Sûreté*, and of his clothes."

"Oh—those . . ."

It was difficult for anyone as large and as aggressive as Rostand to look sheepish, but aided no doubt by M. Pinaud's deliberate and icy incisiveness, he came as near to it as was humanly possible.

"Yes. Those. As you say. Those clothes which you tore and ruined by covering with blood and sausage-meat, to say nothing of suet and entrails, thereby committing wrongful assault with malicious violence."

"Now—now, M'sieu Pinaud," protested the butcher, "you are making a mountain with all those long words out of a very small matter."

Suddenly he grinned and his whole countenance was transfigured.

"All I did was hold him up and roll him over the bench and rub his nose in everything there. You should have seen it—I could hardly find the strength for laughing. But he deserved it—he was so rude and so arrogant. I told him I had no objection to answering questions if they were put in a civil voice, but bumptious little upstarts should always be put in their place."

M. Pinaud hastily put up his hand and smoothed his moustache.

"You are extremely lucky not to have been charged," he said gravely. "Fortunately I happened to be with

M'sieu le Maire at the time, and as a result of our understanding together the whole thing can now be forgotten. By the way, did he have a revolver?"

"No, m'sieu. I would have returned it to you if he had. I am afraid the suit is torn."

"That does not matter. He can afford a new one."

M. Pinaud was glad that M. le Chef did not allow junior detectives to be armed. Otherwise what had turned out to be nothing more than a salutary lesson might well have ended in tragedy.

He cleared his throat in a businesslike fashion.

"Now then, let us get down to business. I am sorry I had to ask you to come here, but I am extremely busy."

"Doing what?" interrupted Rostand scornfully. He had regained all his self-confidence with miraculous rapidity.

M. Pinaud retained his calm.

"Trying to find a murderer," he replied equably. "That is why I asked you to come here."

"So that you could pin it on me."

"No. I don't have to pin a crime, as you put it, on anyone. I am Pinaud. I do not work in that way. I solve the case, and the guilty one is punished."

"You said I was suspect."

"Everyone is suspect—until the case is solved."

"Well, why don't you solve this one?"

"I am doing my best. Where were you last night?"

"Asleep in bed."

"Can you prove it?"

"Of course not. I'm not married. Neither am I courting. Therefore I sleep alone. Therefore it is my word against yours."

"Fair enough. For the moment we will accept it. You have heard, no doubt—since news travels quickly in a small town—that it was M'siu Minoton who was murdered last night?"

"Yes," replied the butcher sullenly. "I had heard. And I am sorry. He was a good man. Why should anyone wish to murder him?"

"Because he had a clue. He was on the track of the murderer."

"Well," replied the butcher rudely, "there is no need to fear for your neck, then."

M. Pinaud ignored this.

"When did you see M'sieu Minoton last?"

"I don't remember. Days ago."

"Did he call to see you yesterday?"

"No. Why are you bothering me in this crazy way?"

M. Pinaud regarded him thoughtfully, puffing out clouds of cigarette smoke reflectively.

"Because I am an extremely puzzled man," he replied slowly. "Because I have a suspect number one and I don't like it. And because you are suspect number two and I don't like that either."

Rostand stared. M. Pinaud's voice had been of such sincerity that it carried conviction.

"Well, you had better take care with all your suspecting and your numbering and your puzzling."

"Why?"

"Because as far as I can see you are likely to end up like M'sieu Minoton."

"That may be. Many have tried but I am still here."

"There is a first time for everything."

"No doubt, but for this one there will be a long wait."

"Look. Why should I be a suspect? I knew Jean Falange, obviously. I quarelled with him—everyone knows that—he was an argumentative type, the sort one quarrels

97

with naturally. But is that a reason for killing a man—because you quarrel with him?

"Nonsense—absolute nonsense. The other man I have never seen before in my life. Why should I murder him? M'sieu Minoton I have known and respected for ten years. But why go on? This is lunacy."

"You are quite right, M'sieu Rostand," replied M. Pinaud calmly. "That is precisely what makes this case so difficult. On the other hand, please remember that you are probably—almost certainly—the only man in town with both the strength and the weapon to explain the singular circumstances of their deaths."

"Nonsense," repeated Rostand the butcher. And this time he did not use the word nonsense. "The fact that I have the strength and the weapon does not necessarily mean that I used them."

"No, not necessarily. But you could have."

"Of course I could have. Who is denying it? But—for the thousandth time get this into your thick head—I did not. I say I did not. I had no reason to. I repeat I did not."

"All right. All right. There is no need to get excited."

"It is enough to excite a dismembered carcass."

"Maybe—but that is just what you are not. At least—not yet. You are a normal intelligent human being. Therefore you must realize that I am only doing my duty. These were routine questions I had to ask you. I regret the necessity of having had to keep you from your shop. You are at liberty to return there now, M'sieu Rostand."

The butcher stared, started to say something, and then turned and went out.

M. Pinaud sighed and lit another cigarette. It was all very confusing.

In the dining-room of the hotel, shadowed and dim in the mellow evening light, a cold meal was laid.

M. Pinaud eyed it appreciatively and speculatively. He was tired and hungry and discouraged, and the tastefully set dishes and the gleaming silver on a spotless cloth went a long way towards soothing his bitterness and frustration.

He took a step nearer. The huge black cat curled up in the armchair opened one sleepy amber eye and regarded him with a mild interest.

There was a note propped up against the bottle of wine. He reached out for it and read the few words scrawled in a large and illiterate hand:

M'sieu, I have had to go out because my father is not well. I hope everything is to your satisfaction and I wish you respectfully a good and hearty appetite.

Annette.

M. Pinaud smiled and for a moment, fleetingly, wonderfully, the harsh and grim lines of his features softened and were transfigured. That would be the plump young girl who had served him before. He hoped sincerely that she was no relation to the dead Dubois, the removal of whose body from the cellar to the morgue he had superintended that very same agternoon It was gratifying to think that in this strange and sometimes horrifying place there were simple and kindly people such as he had been wont to know, and amongst them one who wished him well.

He folded up the paper carefully and placed it in his wallet. From the other side, whose thin emptiness made him sigh, he as carefully extracted a note, folded it in half and tucked it under the edge of a plate. If her father were ill she would be thankful for a little extra.

Then he lifted the cover off one of the dishes and sniffed appreciatively. There were sardines—large ones—fat ones—laid out in an orderly manner between halves of cold hard-boiled egg, and on each egg was a small and delicious looking onion.

The cat began to purr. M. Pinaud looked around. Both eyes were open, no longer sleepy, no longer mildly interested, but blazing now with an amber glow.

M. Pinaud was fond of cats. He remembered the nondescript tabby at home over which his daughters made such an inordinate fuss, and for a moment, fleetingly, poignantly, memory came to touch him with a grieving finger. For a moment he felt the pulse of loneliness; for a moment the true horror of what he was investigating seemed to sear his consciousness like a vivid flame. For a moment he despaired of ever succeeding and wished that he could be home again, home amidst everything that was familiar and dear and happy with the people he loved.

But the moment passed. M. Pinaud sighed and wondered if he were growing old.

Then he tipped a piece of bread off a small plate, took a sardine by its tail and placed it carefully in the middle. Then he set the plate on the armchair in front of the cat.

Then he removed the cover from another dish and contemplated its contents—cold pork chops—with a benign approval.

Finally he drew up a chair and sat down. There were five sardines left and four halves of egg. M. Pinaud looked rapidly around the table. There were three pork chops, a bowl of potato salad, another of lettuce, a Camembert cheese and a loaf of bread.

M. Pinaud delicately detached one more sardine from

the dish and then suddenly froze rigidly, his knife and fork poised in mid-air.

The noise behind him was unmistakable. Terrible and horrible and quite unmistakable.

For a long moment he remained there motionless, with the perspiration drying coldly on his brow, and yet his powerful hands continued to grip the knife and fork without a tremor, such was his iron self-control.

Then at length, when all was quiet, his hands dropped and he turned round slowly in his chair.

The cat was dead, stiff-legged in that last convulsive spasm of agony. The empty plate gleamed pallidly in the dying light.

In the gathering gloom of the dying day M. Pinaud hurried as fast as he could towards the railway station.

Let no one rashly and inaccurately assume that he was running away. That was something he would never do.

But at the moment, and with some justification, he had had enough of the hotel. He argued with a certainty born of long experience that where there was a station there would be a railway inn. Sometimes it was mean, sometimes it was poor and humble, yet nevertheless it would exist, and there he would be able to eat and sleep and perhaps forget that cold fear which still seemed to crouch on his shoulder. There perhaps he would find peace, and an escape from those memories which now walked in his footsteps and hurried with his haste, and surged within his mind to make a mockery of any coherent thought.

At length he came to the station. He had not been mistaken. On the opposite side of the square, sheltering behind the whispering plane trees, stood a small and weatherbeaten inn.

Without hesitation M. Pinaud opened the door, muttered the customary greeting to the few men in the café and walked straight through to the dining room.

With a sigh of relief he sat down at a corner table, grasped a long loaf which lay in a basket and quickly tore off a large piece which he proceeded to masticate with the utmost satisfaction.

"As you will observe," he remarked placidly to the girl who came to stare at him open-mouthed. "As you will have gathered, I am hungry."

"Indeed, m'sieu," she replied with an expression of the greatest interest and without the trace of a smile, "one would have been perfectly justified in concluding that you were starving."

"Not quite," conceded M. Pinaud, tearing off another large portion of bread, "but well on the way to starvation. Now let us cease this idle conversation, which may be all very well in its place, but which is useless in satisfying my hunger. Bring me something to eat, as soon as you can. And I would like to sleep here tonight, if you have a room."

"Certainly, m'sieu."

In a remarkably short time she reappeared with a carafe of wine and a large bowl of soup, fragrant and steaming. With this she had the foresight to bring another loaf, so that in a short while the first and most immediate pangs of M. Panaud's hunger were allayed.

With the bowl empty and the comforting glow of the soup warm in his belly, M. Pinaud sat back in his chair and tried to think, calmly and logically.

The initial shock by now had worn off. Once again he

was master of himself. But not, as he was the first to admit, master of the situation. Not by any means. Once again he had no proof.

The door of the hotel was always left open on the latch; anyone could have come in after the girl Annette had gone. Perhaps her father was not ill at all; a message to that effect would have ensured a clear field and ample time and opportunity. Once again he was back to where he had started the night before, fighting an unknown adversary who was ruthlessly determined to exterminate him regardless of the consequences.

And would there be any consequences?

M. Pinaud contemplated the enormous escalope on his plate with a gloomy satisfaction.

Normally, and under any other circumstances, the extermination of a member of the *Sûreté*, and particularly of such a member as M. Pinaud, would be fraught with the most unpleasant consequences for whoever attempted such a misdeed.

But here in Chassagne, M. Pinaud remembered with a sudden and extremely distasteful clarity—here in Chassagne heads were severed from their respective bodies with an altogether horrifying and frightening ease and—as the murderer was no doubt in the habit of arguing with a completely satisfying and altogether unanswerable logic—once a head is removed from its body there is a certain difficulty in initiating any consequences or retribution or punishment.

M. Pinaud attacked his escalope with determination. After all, he was still hungry; that was the important thing to remember.

As he wielded knife and fork firmly he cast his mind

back, striving to make sure out of what had happened, seeking for the key which would unravel the mystery.

Both Roland Capt and Rostand the butcher had been in town that day. Either of them would have had the opportunity to visit the hotel in the afternoon. And similarly, either of them could have bribed Dubois to attempt what on the face of it appeared a perfectly simple operation. It was not likely that Dubois had acted on his own initiative. Innkeepers do not usually make a practice of attempting to murder their guests; such a habit could hardly be expected to result in an increase in their custom.

M. Pinaud regarded his empty plate thoughtfully. Then he raised his eyes and smiled as he saw the girl standing in front of him. She set down on the table the half of a large plum tart, together with a clean plate.

M. Pinaud thanked her politely, pushed the plate to one side and drew the dish nearer. After all, why give her more washing-up?

The important thing was that the attempts had been made. Which meant that the murderer was getting anxious—the murderer would feel happier with M. Pinaud out of the way.

M. Pinaud sighed—let it be confessed—with an expression of complacent satisfaction.

Someone must have heard of Pinaud. Even in the remote backwoods of this lost corner of France some echo of that almost superhuman fame must have penetrated. Elsewhere it was known that M. Pinaud never gave up until he had succeeded—that the failures and discouragements and setbacks and reverses which would put an end to any normal individual's activities had no effect on him except to strengthen his determination to succeed. Failure, he would often say, is nothing but the opportunity to try again, a little more intelligently. These things were known in the civilized world. It was a comforting and a gratifying thought, particularly in the midst of all this horror and mystery, to reflect that their import was spreading even to the most primitive parts of the country.

M. Pinaud nodded as if in confirmation of this eminently gratifying reflection and scraped the last mouthfuls of tart from the dish. Perhaps there would be some cheese.

Then he sighed. This speculation was interesting, but of singularly little value. He was concerned with facts, and facts were the things he did not have. In the morning he would go again to the *château*. It was there that the whole thing had started. Perhaps there he would find a clue.

The girl brought him a large dish with four varieties of cheese on it. M. Pinaud thanked her and asked if she would mind bringing another loaf, so that he might do justice to them all.

Once he had finished he would go to bed. It had been a tiring day.

Chapter Eight

IN the morning it was Marie Capt who met him at the door of the Château, her eyes dark pools of suffering in the pallid oval of the face.

"Come in, M'sieu Pinaud, I am glad you came. I wanted to see you. But please excuse me for a moment, I must telephone for Armand. My mother—she is bad this morning."

"Of course. Take your time, mademoiselle. I can wait."

M. Pinaud's face was grave. There were times when he hated his duty.

She showed him into a small room on the far side of the vast hall and left him for a few moments. During the whole of that time M. Pinaud remained exactly where he had halted, without moving, without relaxing. His eyes were open, but they saw nothing.

When she returned he lifted his head and seemed to make a great effort to rouse imself.

"You know why I have come, I suppose," he said quietly.

"No—I have no idea. And I don't care. I only know that you said you would help—you promised to do your best. And now after this horrible thing yesterday—this killing of M'sieu Minoton—we need you more than ever. I did not have the opportunity of seeing you when you were here—I came to the hotel last night and waited for hours, but you had gone—no one knew where, and I waited and waited.   "

Suddenly her voice broke and she buried her face in her hands. With infinite gentleness M. Pinaud put an arm around her shoulders.

"There, now—don't cry. I am sorry you had to wait for nothing. I did not dream you would come, or else I would have been there."

The words he said were nothing It is doubtful if she heard or understood them. But the comfort and the kindness in that deep voice seemed to reach out and gather her distress and her grief and enfold them with a warmth and a tenderness that was like a soothing and healing balm.

After a while she looked up, with the tears still glistening in her eyes, and M. Pinaud caught his breath in a swift surge of emotion at the wonder of her beauty.

In her youth and her loveliness there were harmonies that seemed like the echoes of forgotten dreams. In that long moment as he watched her M. Pinaud's thoughts were confused and lonely, and sad with a poignant and somehow terrible wistfulness.

It was a long time since he had dreamed. It was a long time since he had been young and filled with the sublime self-confidence of youth, able to meet life with a jest and a song in the knowledge—strong and vital and compelling —that he could challenge it unafraid and if necessary change it and mould it to conform to his heart's desire. That had been a long time ago.

And now it seemed that he stood once more in the midst of his dreams. He felt their wonder all about him. They seemed to surge up inside him as he looked at her, until it was as if the mellow autumn sunshine came not from without but from within. Now it seemed that his dreams were all about him, and yet he knew that he had no part in them, since he had dreamed them all so long ago. He had no right to them. He was no longer the young man who had created them. He was what life and the passing of the years had made him.

And in that thought there was no bitterness, only a poignancy and a wistfulness at the memory of their beauty.

"Thank you," she said simply.

M. Pinaud sighed.

"You know," he said heavily, "you realize that I have no alternative but to arrest Roland."

"No—no!" she breathed, her eyes widening in horror. "You don't mean that—you couldn't. . . ."

"I am sorry, mademoiselle. Believe me, I am sorry. And I do not want to do it. Within me I do not feel that I should. And yet it seems that I have no other alternative. The evidence is only circumstantial, but it is overwhelming."

"That is what we have always dreaded; that has always been our fear," she said in a very quiet voice, "ever since the first body—that of Jean Falange—was found in the garden. I shall never forget the expression in my mother's eyes as she looked from the body to Roland—I could see her heart breaking beneath the words she did not dare to say."

"She knew, then."

"No—no!" Marie cried fiercely. "She did not know anything, and she did not dare to guess. She is his mother. I just had to stand there and watch her heart breaking with the fear and the uncertainty and the suspicion. And when the second one was found in the same way——"

"What do you mean—in the same way?"

"It was found in the garden—almost in the same place. That time I thought she would die. But she would not give in. She got Rostand to carry it away in his van and put it on the railway line; he would do anything for her."

"I see now," muttered M. Pinaud.

"You can see why we were so terrified when you suddenly appeared with that body in your car—and ever since we have been living in a nightmare. That is why she told you all that nonsense about Rostand and the Mayor—she was only trying to take your mind off Roland. She knows he is innocent, just as I know he is innocent. But we both know what people will think. How many persons are convicted each year on circumstantial evidence?"

"I don't know—hundreds."

"Yes—so you see what I mean."

For a moment there was silence, and then M. Pinaud shook his head as if bewildered.

"If only I knew how . . ." he muttered.

Her interruption came with the quickness of a sword-thrust.

"But there is no question of how—I tell you he didn't do it. He couldn't have done such a thing; he is incapable of such violence and horror."

M. Pinaud looked at her thoughtfully.

"You really believe that, don't you? You really believe that he is innocent."

"Of course I do."

"And Madame your mother believes in him as well."

"Yes, but she is getting old. It is the uncertainty and the not-knowing which is killing her—the knowledge that she cannot ask him—the thought that if she did he might deny it in good faith not knowing himself. You know that he has spells when—when he is not . . ."

"Yes," said M. Pinaud gently, "you mother told me about those."

"She told you about those she knows, when she can look after him. Now she is tormented by the thought that perhaps there are others that she doesn't know—perhaps there are others that he himself doesn't know."

Her voice, in all its quiet bitterness, suddenly ceased and she began to tremble. Once again M. Pinaud laid a hand on her shoulders to comfort her. Once again the deep voice, infinitely kind and gentle, came to soothe and comfort her.

"Leave this to me," he said slowly, "I will wait a little longer. There may be something I have overlooked—something I should have seen. Give me a little more time.

I would like to search the whole place, if you don't mind, very thoroughly."

"Of course not—do as you please. And now if you will excuse me, I must go to her."

"Naturally. I will see you later."

M. Pinaud came out to the stone steps. The doctor's Bugatti was parked in the drive. He walked round to the back of the house and stood there for a moment, lost in meditation.

It was difficult to believe that here were both horror and violence.

The vast old Château seemed to sleep, tranquil with the peace of centuries, its open balcony gay with its sun-blinds and flowers, its massive stone walls hidden beneath the curling vines and clinging peaches, the shuttered windows staring like bright blind eyes, patient in the haze of the mellow autumn sunshine. On their perches the doves murmured, *rou-crou, rou-crou,* and high above his head a bird soared, a fluttering speck in the wide blue sky.

Beyond the walled garden lay the orchards and the farm. Beyond them the vineyards and the forests and all the rolling countryside that the first Hugues Capt had bequeathed to his relatives to ensure his hold on the fair land of France.

This was the tragedy. M. Pinaud was a sensitive and an imaginative man, and this he could understand. That such a glorious continuity, which had outlasted the centuries, should end in this way, with the heir to such a heritage incarcerated for the rest of his life—that was the tragedy. A tragedy almost as great as the deeds whereby this had come about.

M. Pinaud sighed. Then, grimly and with a kind of

savage despair, he began to search the whole place—the house, the outbuildings, the garden and even the orchards and the farm. He searched with a thoroughness born of the intensity of his own prejudice and of the passionate conviction in Marie Capt's voice, which seemed to resound through his mind long after she had gone.

He did not really know for what he was looking; he had no idea what he expected to find. But, characteristically, he gave all his energies to the task, not sparing himself, not even pausing to rest.

As he came out on the long balcony he saw the ladder at the far end, leading up to the roof. From his previous visits he remembered that the room at the end, with its long french windows, was the one in which Madame Capt had first received him.

Walking quietly, he traversed the length of the balcony. In the corner a brazier glowed and a crucible of molten lead bubbled on the hot coals. M. Pinaud grasped the rungs of the ladder and climbed swiftly to the roof.

An old man, with a seamed and weatherbeaten face, was straddling the tiles.

"What are you doing here?" asked M. Pinaud.

The old man stared at him belligerently.

"I might ask the same question," he retorted. "And that is my ladder—you have no right to climb it without asking my permission."

M. Pinaud felt in his pocket and produced his badge and his official card.

"My name is Pinaud—from the *Sûreté*. I am not in the mood for insolence. Answer my question civilly or it will be the worse for you."

"I am sorry, m'sieu," replied the old man meekly, "but

you must admit that it is a bit of a shock when someone climbs your ladder without——"

"All right, all right, so it is your ladder and I climbed it. Now what are young doing here?"

The old man's stare plainly implied that no one could possibly be so ignorant.

"Why—as you see, m'sieu—I am mending the roof. That is my job. I have always mended this roof, ever since I was a boy. My father taught me how. He had it from his father who had it from his father who had it——"

"All right—I see what you mean. It is a family craft."

"That's it, that's it. But who is going to mend it when I am gone? I have no son—at least, I had one—but he did not come back . . ."

The old man's high-pitched drawl quivered uncertainly and then stopped. M. Pinaud, although he was in a hurry, waited sympathetically while the old man blew his nose violently on a huge red handkerchief.

"How long have you been doing this—I mean, when did you begin?"

"A few days ago."

"What time do you start in the mornings?"

"Oh—about eleven. I have to cook my breakfast first, and that takes time. I am not as quick as I used to be. Mam'zelle Marie is always complaining. Antoine, she says to me—how is it going? I tell her it is going along —going along nicely, and she says it has been going along nicely for far too many days, and then I say—do you know what I say, m'sieu?"

M. Pinaud had already begun to descend the ladder.

"No, what do you say?"

"I say that most things have a habit of doing that, and there are not many men left in the world who can repair

112

a lead roof five hundred years old. That usually puts an end to her impatience."

"I see what you mean," replied M. Pinaud, as his head disappeared below the level of the gutter.

Quickly he opened the wooden door at the end of the balcony and descended the steps into the garden. Here he was wasting his time. If the old man had come to work early he might have seen or heard something, but by eleven o'clock even the bodies had been removed.

He expected to find Roland in the barn, but the building was empty. M. Pinaud spent some time in looking at everything very carefully. The forge at the far end seemed to interest him particularly, but apart from an unfinished pair of wrought-iron gates and some agricultural implements he did not find anything to indicate that it had been put to any other use.

Out in the garden again, he saw the figure of Victoire the housekeeper descending the wooden steps from the balcony with a basket on her arm, and walked to meet her.

"Good morning, m'sieu," she said politely, her severe and forbidding countenance clearly expressing her disapproval.

For a moment M. Pinaud grinned impishly.

"At least this time it is too late to call," he reminded her cheerfully, and waited in vain for some change of expression on the grimly austere countenance. But she just continued to look at him.

"Did you wish to speak to me, m'sieu? I was about to pick some flowers."

M. Pinaud's grin vanished. He walked with her down the garden, away from the house.

"Yes. Tell me—there are three in the family, and yourself. Any more?"

"No, m'sieu. Two girls come in daily from Chassagne to help with the housework."

"And here there must be some thirty rooms, at least. Are they used?"

"No, m'sieu. Most of them are closed."

"Those at the far end there—on the ground floor——"

It was at that precise moment that they heard Marie Capt scream.

M. Pinaud bit off what he had been saying and ran as fast as he could towards the house. He looked up and saw the french windows at the end of the balcony were open, and so he climbed the wooden steps which led there from the garden.

They were all there, grouped about the still and silent figure in the armchair—Dr. Reuge, Marie, Roland and old Antoine, his weatherbeaten features tear-stained and grim.

For a moment they all stood looking at him in silence, and then Victoire pushed by his side with a cry of dismay and the spell was broken.

Marie Capt looked longer than the others. Her voice trembled, but otherwise she seemed remarkably composed.

"I am sorry I screamed. Did I startle you?"

"You startled me," put in Antoine hoarsely. "I was on the roof and when I heard that scream I came down my ladder as fast as I could."

M. Pinaud shook his head.

"There is no need to apologize. How did it happen?"

Dr. Reuge stepped forward, a syringe still in his hand.

"There is very little to say, m'seu. Her heart just gave out under the pain. I was actually putting some warm

114

oil in her ear when I saw that she had collapsed. I tried an injection of strychnine, but it was useless."

"Had she suffered long from this abscess?"

"Yes—for over a week. There was little I could do, except put in warm oil and wait for it to burst. I gave her morphia tablets for the pain."

"She would not take them," put in Marie.

"I know. I could not force her."

"She said that if she had to suffer she would endure it."

"She was a great lady," said M. Pinaud simply and sincerely. "People are no longer cast in the same mould. Mademoiselle—and you too, M'sieu Capt—I offer you my deepest sympathy."

"Thank you, m'sieu," said Marie.

Roland did not answer. He had been standing beside the armchair all the time, without moving. M Pinaud could not read his expression since his eyes were looking down.

"And mine, too," added Dr. Reuge. "We must look on it as a merciful release. The inflammation was acute— she must have suffered greatly. And her heart has been weak ever since I have known her."

"Yes," said Marie slowly, "I suppose you are right. It helps if one thinks of it in that way—that at last she is now at rest. Come, Roland. . . ."

She held out her hand towards her brother. Roland did not move. She took a step towards him and touched his arm. He turned slowly and came towards her, the agony in his features terrible to see.

Gently, and with touching compassion, she led him from the room.

Antonine muttered something unintelligible and walked

out to the balcony. Victoire went blindly through the door, clutching her apron to her eyes.

M. Pinaud and the doctor were left facing each other in the silent room.

M. Pinaud felt absent-mindedly for his cigarettes, and then dug his hands fiercely into his pockets.

"It would seem that there is a curse on this house," he observed.

Dr. Reuge nodded gloomily.

"First one thing, and then another. You are right. This —is not surprising."

"What do you mean?"

"The shock of these other things, and thinking what they implied. It is a wonder her heart lasted until today."

M. Pinaud rubbed his chin reflectively.

"I don't know. That is not altogether accurate. The shock of finding those bodies here—yes—and the shock of what others would think—maybe—but she always believed him innocent. And so, for that matter, does his sister. That is what worries me."

Dr. Reuge busied himself replacing his stethoscope and his syringe in his bag.

"That I find perfectly natural," he said. "That is what his mother and his sister would think."

"But you do not agree?"

The doctor shrugged.

"How can I? I have doctored so many since the war— broken bodies and broken limbs—and those without a mark or a scar on them. Those are the worst. Doctors prate about penicillin and blood plasma and all the wonders with which science can save the soldier's body, but they have not dared to cross the threshold and look at what war does to a man's mind. I stood in a tent for sixteen hours at a stretch, operating without anaesthetics and without antiseptics after an air-raid. Some of them lived. Some of them lived to be idiots. I could not operate on their minds."

He closed the bag abruptly.

"Did you get my report?"

M. Pinaud nodded thoughtfully.

"Yes, thank you. It is of no use—you realize that?"

"Naturally. The same as the others. When is your Vinet arriving?"

"He should have been here today. Mind you, it is a long shot. I don't for a moment suppose he will find anything."

"Well, it is worth trying. And now if you will excuse me, I have things to prepare here."

"Of course. I will go back to town. I must telephone Paris."

Chapter Nine

AFTER M. Pinaud had finished his various telephone calls, which took him some time, he went back to the inn, and being a logical and methodical man, he took off all his clothes before going to bed.

In the middle of one of his more heated discussions with M. le Chef he suddenly remembered that what with all the unexpectedness and excitement of Madame Capt's death he had completely forgotten to continue his search of the Château. Now he remembered his conversation with Victoire, and the thought of all those unoccupied rooms intrigued him.

He thought that it would be better if he went later, under cover of darkness, and with a swift thrill of entirely unjustified and yet nevertheless definite anticipation, he considered it preferable to approach this task refreshed as far as possible both in body and in mind.

He therefore placed his head on the pillow and in a moment was sleeping as peacefully as a child.

He had a happy faculty of complete detachment; having decided that he might be up half the night, he knew that he would need sleep in order to concentrate all his faculties successfully. With a deliberate effort of will he closed his mind to all his doubts and all his perplexities and all his worries, and for a moment thought about his wife and his children and his home. As always, such thoughts brought a familiar and comforting sense of peace and achievement, for M. Pinaud could still remember the days when he despaired of ever possessing any of these things.

Beneath that peace surged the fatigue inevitably engendered by the days of suspense and anxiety, and just before the waves of lassitude rose up to engulf him—in that momentary hush when sleep surged soundlessly and silently onwards—M. Pinaud thanked the good God for his mercies to him and requested humbly that He bless his home and cherish the people he loved within it.

Then he fell asleep.

Later that evening M. Pinaud, fully clothed and very wide awake, knocked on the door of Charles Valin's room.

"Come in."

M. Pinaud went in. M. Pinaud stared in amazement. Charles Valin, in a brocaded dressing-gown over silk pyjamas and with a nightcap on his head, was sitting on the bed manicuring his finger-nails.

The dressing-gown M. Pinaud could understand. That kept out the cold. The silk pyjamas too; apparently the silk was warm and pleasant to wear, if one could afford the price. The finger-nails too, presented no difficulty to his intelligence. While it was not a habit in which he himself had ever indulged, at least it was preferable to the displaying of dirt-encrusted talons so favoured by the younger generation of today.

But the nightcap he simply could not understand. After all, it was not yet winter—surely it could not be to keep out the cold.

However, being a man of innate tact and instinctive good manners, he kept his thoughts to himself.

"I am sorry to disturb you so late," he began.

"That is all right, m'sieu, I had not gone to bed."

"How did you get on today?"

Charles Valin grimaced.

"Wasting time, I am afraid. And you?"

"Well, you heard about M'sieu Minoton?"

"Yes."

"Naturally, I questioned them at the Château."

And briefly M. Pinaud recounted the sum total of his activities that day, including the death of Madame Capt.

"Somehow it always seems to come back to the Château," he added in conclusion. "I feel that so strongly that I propose to go back there now and finish my search. I gave most of it a fairly thorough examination today, but I was interrupted by all the excitement over the old lady's death. I noticed that there were some unoccupied rooms at one end; I would like to have a look at those. Would you care to come with me?"

Charles Valin stared.

"What—now?"

"Yes Now is the time. We shall not be disturbed."

If Charles Valin hesitated, it was only for a second. After all, to be asked to accompany the great Pinaud on his investigations was not an honour which befell anybody, not even a relative of the Minister.

"I shall be delighted. Give me a couple of minutes to get dressed."

"Of course. I will wait for you outside in my car."

M. Pinaud paused with one hand on the door. Charles Valin's feet were elegant in Spanish morocco slippers. Beside the bed, wooden trees reposed snugly in a pair of exquisite hand-sewn brogues. M. Pinaud looked down at his own square-toed boots and sighed.

And yet all this he could understand. This was only the result of money and the privilege of having plenty. This was something which had never bothered him, since he had never had enough to spare.

But about the nightcap—that was odd. That was definitely inexplicable.

For a moment curiosity fought with his good manners and then curiosity won. He pointed with one finger.

"Excuse me for asking—but why?"

Charles Valin looked at him swiftly and shrewdly—at his ill-fitting and crumpled suit, his heavy boots and his thatch of unkempt hair—and behind it all, being of a sensitive nature, he saw the kindliness and the simplicity and the innate goodness which made the man what he was. And beneath that goodness he sensed the strength and the indomitable purpose of his character, and he remembered how M. Pinaud had championed him and defeated M. le Maire for his sake the day before.

And therefore, being—in spite of all his money and his consanguinity with the Minister—a young man of fundamentally sound quality, he replied with a perfectly serious face, in a grave and courteous manner, as one would impart information to an inhabitant of another world.

"That is to keep the wave in the hair, m'sieu, when the head is laid on the pillow at night."

M. Pinaud drove the car slowly and carefully to the side of the disused gatehouse, where he switched off the engine and extinguished the lights.

"I think I had better go first," he said. "Give me five minutes and then join me. Straight up the drive and round to the back of the house. I will be in the garden there, waiting for you. Keep to the shadows in case anyone should be up and watching."

"Very well, m'sieu."

Then, walking quietly on the grass verge so that his footsteps would not sound on the gravel, M. Pinaud made his way up the drive towards the Château.

The moon was full, a mellow autumn moon that seemed to ride the vast sea of the sky with a tranquil, gliding ease. M. Pinaud kept in the shelter of the bushes as much as possible, and when he came to the Château he slipped unobserved through the dark shadows of the walls until he came to the garden at the back of the house.

There he could no longer take cover. The garden was almost as bright as day. He noticed that there was a light in the barn.

Then he looked around him. The house slept, tranquil and undisturbed. The moonlight drenched the whole scene with a clear unearthly radiance greying the white shutters, silvering the grey stone walls, and glistening over the lead tiles with a blue metallic sheen. The wonder and the beauty of it all came to grip him in a swift sudden surge of emotion.

M. Pinaud was a sensitive and an imaginative man. For a moment he stood there, alone in the bright moon-drenched wonder of the night, oblivious of his mission and his duty and his purpose, while his heart and his mind seemed to unfold together in one vast surge of understanding and sympathy.

Dark was the ivy beneath the roof, and in the breeze its pattern of darkness seemed to heave, sending ripples of shadow over the bulk of the massive walls, leaning a little with age, which made two sides of that vast rectangle which was the house.

Those rough-hewn stones had heard prayers for the Crusades; they had seen a Capt ride off for Jerusalem and the farm-wain creaking down the dusty road to the cobbles of Paris and the guillotine. They had heard violins playing a minuet from the minstrels' gallery above the hall, and listened to the screams of the peasants whom the men-at-arms flogged for not paying *al gabee.*

They had seen spearmen and axemen and pikemen, priests and cardinals, warriors and clerks, wainwrights and armourers, jugglers and tumblers, stone-masons and carpenters; they had seen men kill each other in the cold grey light of dawn for an academic point of honour.

On the Eve of St. Bartholomew a Capt had died with his back to that wall, parrying for mad and glorious moments the blades that flickered before the white arm-lets of shame. Those stones had watched the fair-haired Saxons march by, flushed with the triumph of Sedan, and the Renault taxis filled with cheering soldiers had swayed and lurched along that steeply cambered road on their way to the Marne.

Not so long ago they had seen the armoured divisions thundering down that same road—the bleak-eyed fanatics sitting impassive in the fumes of diesel oil, with their automatic weapons ready in their hands and the pride of conquest in the lift of their heads. They had taught the world a new lesson—this was only another country, the ancient enemy, who would also have to learn. The lesson had many pages—some lived a part in Oslo or Copenhagen and some died in the choking chlorine-filled hull of a submarine—some bombed the streets of Rotterdam while others slid with their grenades in their teeth down the ventilator-shafts of the forts at Maestricht—but the core of the book was stark and hard and the young men believed in it.

This was a house of history, a house that had aged with the history of France, a house that had known bloodshed and endeavour and suffering and folly—and a pride and a dignity which always transcended them, and had mellowed with the passing of the centuries in which that history had been written. This was a house that had grown old with the passing of time and proud with the changing of the years.

And now, in the evening of its life, this horror had come upon it. Suddenly M. Pinaud shivered as if with cold. Standing there alone in the moonlight, he shivered. The night was not cold, but fear seemed to touch him with an icy finger.

Before, he had looked at the house as a whole and allowed his imagination to run riot. Now he looked at it again, carefully and factually, noting and observing each detail.

In that brief moment in which he stood there watching intently, the silence seemed to surge outward and spread, indefinably, until it was as if it became part of the moonlight, part of that bright unreal mystery, part of the magic and the beauty of the night.

And then Charles Valin laid a hand on his arm and the spell was broken.

"Good," he whispered. "Very good indeed. I did not hear you come."

This, from M. Pinaud, was praise indeed.

"Thank you, m'sieu," muttered Charles Valin.

In that moment of intense watchfulness M. Pinaud had noticed something unusual.

"Look," he said quietly, pointing with one hand, "look at that end room on the ground floor . . ."

"There is no window."

"The shutters were closed this morning, when she told me that the wing was not used."

"They are open now—and hooked back too."

For a moment M. Pinaud hesitated.

"Let me go, m'sieu," said Charles Valin.

"Very well."

After all, this was something that he could do. So far the case had hardly been an interesting one for him.

Quickly and silently they crossed the intervening space. Charles Valin reached up with his hands on the sill and looked inside.

M. Pinaud went on round the corner of the house. From the opposite wall he heard a faint rustling sound, but when he came back to stand close behind Charles Valin he could see nothing but impenetrable shadow.

The tall window appeared to have no glass. The moonlight flooded the empty room with a pale and unearthly radiance.

But it was not quite empty. Even from where he stood,

M. Pinaud could see by the far wall, ranged neatly in line, the buckets of water.

Suddenly the significance of Charles Valin's position flooded him with horror—his head over the sill, his fingers together, clutching the wood.

He wondered if there were deep grooves beneath the delicately manicured fingers, and even as he opened his mouth to ask he felt sick and faint with realization and understanding.

And in that same instant he heard the hiss of the falling blade.

His reflexes obeyed his instinctive reaction with instantaneous speed and his powerful hands shot out, dug into the young man's shoulders and tore him away from the window with a fraction of a second to spare.

Even so, he could have sworn that he felt the cold breath of the heavy steel blade on his brow as it thudded down into the wood.

For a long moment M. Pinaud leaned against the wall, unable to move, agonized and powerless as if in the panic of a nightmare. The narrowness of Charles Valin's escape affected him, strangely enough, as strongly as if it were he himself who had experienced it.

For a long moment they just stayed there, spent and shaking, the one grateful that he was alive, the other thankful that he had been able to save him.

The massive rough-hewn stones behind M. Pinaud's back gave him reassurance; their solidity and their strength had endured for so long that their rocklike impregnability seemed eternal. Strangely, the thought comforted him. Men were born to sorrow and men died—suddenly, peacefully or bloodily—but when men built well, their work endured.

Had Charles Valin not escaped this wall and this house would still have endured, out-reaching life, outlasting death.

He groped in his pockets for his cigarettes and lighter. His fingers were still trembling so much that he had the greatest difficulty in spinning the wheel, but after he had inhaled the smoke deeply several times the worst effects of the reaction began to pass, and as the moments slipped by and he still stood there silently smoking, he felt himself again.

"Well," he said quietly. "Now we know how it was done."

He offered his packet of cigarettes to Charles Valin. The young man's face was ghastly in the moonlight. He did not answer, but reached out eagerly for a cigarette. M. Pinaud lit it from the glowing end of his own.

"It just shows," M. Pinaud continued musingly, "how one should always persevere, even when things seem hopeless. I could have sworn that I had explored every avenue, that I had neglected nothing. And then I said to myself—there must be something more. There must be something I have not seen. And so I decided to search. And here is the result—appalling but magnificent."

Charles Valin did not answer. M. Pinaud continued, warming himself at the fire of his own eloquence:

"Naturally I am thankful that you escaped, but had I failed, it is comforting to reflect that at least you would have had the privilege of dying in the cause of justice. M. le Chef would have been gratified, I can assure you.

"I shall make a point of informing him of the valuable contribution your efforts have made towards the solving of this case. Were it not for the fact that you volunteered to examine the window and by standing there enabled me to realize the significance of your position and solve the mystery of the severed finger-tips, we might still be in the dark. Mind you, in all modesty I shall be compelled to add to my report how my realization was translated into action with a celerity which I think I can fairly claim did me no discredit, for had this not been so, any reward you may have merited would have been somewhat difficult to collect with your head severed from your body and your finger-tips——"

At this juncture in his monologue the knees of Charles Valin buckled suddenly and the body of Charles Valin pitched backwards in a dead faint, and the face of Charles Valin, ghastly white, glimmered pallidly and rigidly in the moonlight.

M. Pinaud sighed philosophically. After all it was not surprising. It is only with age and the passing of the years, each one with its own gradual and subtle and imperceptible immunization, that such shocks can be borne with equanimity and patience and calmness and tranquillity and fortitude.

From now on, he was on his own.

He knew that he needed a drink. He knew that he had never desired or longed for a drink in his life as much as at this moment, but with characteristic single-mindedness he resolutely fought the temptation.

There was work to be done. He was on duty. This escape had been in the normal course of duty. After all, it had been tried before, on two occasions. And yet somehow, M. Pinaud thought as he extinguished the butt of his cigarette with a massive iron-tipped heel, pushing a man down a vertical flight of steps or poisoning him did not seem in any way as horrible as severing his head, suddenly and awfully and completely, with one stroke of a heavy steel blade. . . .

The drink could wait.

M. Pinaud turned and examined the window. The blade, which was razor-sharp and beautifully forged, was weighted with flat bars of iron, and worked on the simple drop principle of the guillotine. The panelling at the top of the window had been hollowed to receive it exactly so that nothing would be visible at a first upward glance. Two rollers at each end of the blade fitted into vertical grooves at the sides to control the drop in one straight line.

M. Pinaud tried to lift the blade; it was as much as he could manage.

A thin strong cord was fastened through a ring at one end, above the weights. M. Pinaud assumed that this would pass over a wheel concealed in the aperture at the top of the window, and pulled taut, would hold the blade in position until required. Then a simple release mechanism, or a trip line, or even cutting the actual retaining cord at another place—and the weight of the blade would do the rest. It was simple and ingenious and, as he had cause to know, diabolically effective.

M. Pinaud wiped the perspiration from his brow and peered thoughtfully into the room.

Then he shook his head and knelt down on the gravel path outside the window. He did not know how the others had been induced to look—perhaps the shutters had simply been opened and curiosity, as in his own case, had done the rest, but it would obviously be easier if the release were actuated from the outside.

M. Pinaud explored with his fingers. The gravel was

thick and deep and sandy—ideal for absorbing the blood. Most of the blood would come from the trunk. The head would not bleed so much—that would be inside. Hence the buckets of water. It was all so fantastically simple and logical—once you knew the answer.

And the finger-tips would either fall inwards into the room or remain on the wood of the sill. There would be no need to hunt for finger-tips in the gravel, digging and scrabbling as he was doing now—perhaps in the darkness when the moon was not bright—what if he touched a finger-tip now? Some of this gravel fell sticky and damp. . . .

M. Pinaud shivered and withdrew his fingers with a sudden savage heave. He needed that drink. More than anything he needed that drink—before his nerves began to scream and he became hysterical.

But as before, obstinately, single-mindedly, magnificently he fought for self-control. Still on his knees, with the perspiration streaming from his face and his heart thudding at the vividness of his imagination, he grimly resisted the temptation to run away from that accursed place and drink the finer edge of his perceptions away.

You are Pinaud, he reminded himself silently and yet forcefully. You have made yourself a career out of nothing. You have created a somebody from a nobody. You are not yet at the summit of that career. You have built yourself a reputation. That has meant hard work and attention to detail. Now you have that reputation to maintain, which means infinitely harder work and the memorizing, classifying and the utilizing of all detail.

This is but one of our many cases. There have been other ones before and there will be more in the future, And this one is not yet ended. This is not the time to weaken, nor to take refuge in drink. The good God helped you to pull that boy's head away just now for a purpose, so that you could use the brains inside your own. Looking at life through the bottom of a glass may make it appear more desirable, but it will not help your brain to function. Come on—find that cord.

Having thus exhorted and encouraged himself with the exuberance of his own eloquence, M. Pinaud dug his fingers once again into the gravel and probed and scrabbled with such diligence that in a short while he found what he was looking for—a thin conduit of wood which obviously contained the cord.

Standing up, he examined the side of the window. After a moment he located the cord, which had been skilfully concealed in a groove made by chiselling out some of the crumbling mortar between the rough-hewn stones. To a casual glance it was invisible.

Since he knew what he was looking for, it was not long before he found it. The cord ran in its crevice at right angles to the window for a metre until it reached an ancient leaden drain-pipe, behind which a small pulley had been fixed. Over this it ran down to the ground, concealed and invisible behind the pipe.

M. Pinaud estimated the direction of the conduit and crossed the narrow lawn unhesitatingly until he came to the high stone wall which enclosed that side of the garden.

As he reached the earth he came into its shadow, and for a moment his eyes, accustomed to the moonlight, could see nothing. Then, as he knelt to explore the earth, he remembered that he had stood there in the sunshine with Victoire that same morning and he remembered the magnificent vine which covered most of that wall, its stems trained and tied to a hand-beaten trellis of iron, drooping and trailing beneath the weight of the great clusters of purple grapes.

The shadow of that high wall would afford perfect cover for someone waiting and watching there, body pressed back against the vine, feet quiet on the soft earth. . . .

M. Pinaud's hands dug swiftly and powerfully, first to one side and then to the other.

It did not take him long to locate it. As he had conjectured, the conduit ran in a straight line across and under the lawn.

Quickly he cleared the earth from the wood. It ran straight towards the wall and then ended, half a metre from the stone.

M. Pinaud reached out his hand and felt. An iron ring had been driven into the stone, just above ground level.

The release was simple. A sharp knife to sever the cord—which was pulled taut when the blade was up and then fastened to the ring—and the weight and the force of gravity did the rest. Another stroke of the knife, and the severed end could be removed, leaving only an empty ring and a conduit which no one would find until they started to dig. And one does not usually dig at the roots of a centuries-old vine.

It was simple—simple and diabolically ingenious.

Chapter Ten

M. PINAUD walked to the barn. The doors were open, the lights on. Roland Capt was working in front of the bench, filing a square on a bar of iron clamped in the vice. He worked quickly and competently, holding the file with loose and practised ease and pausing frequently to examine what he had done.

M. Pinaud came nearer.

"Good evening, m'sieu, how are you?" he said.

Roland turned with a start and nearly dropped the file.

"M'sieu Pinaud, what on earth are you doing here at this hour?"

"I am investigating," replied M. Pinaud, fumbling in his pocket for his cigarettes. "But I might ask you the same question."

Above the flame of his lighter his eyebrows lifted quizzically. Roland laughed easily, without embarrassment.

"I was working on these gates with Dr. Reuge. It is not an easy task and I was glad of his help."

"He is not here now?"

"Oh no. He left some time ago to see a patient. I thought I might as well finish them and so I kept on. I did not realize it was so late. But now I have only the hinges to finish."

M. Pinaud eyed him thoughtfully. He was intent and eager, absorbed and interested in his work. If he was acting, his talents were consummate. There were one or two wooden-handled knives on the bench. He was wearing his usual spotless white shirt, but he could easily have flung on a dark jacket over that before going out.

And yet M. Pinaud did not believe that he was acting. To one who had seen the life and the intelligence die from those alert dark eyes, the enthusiasm and the interest in them now compelled attention and belief. This was normality for him; this was the relief and the reality of self-expression. This was the sheet-anchor in the sea of doubt

132

and depression and mystery. On the other hand, perhaps there was no need to act. Perhaps he did not know. Perhaps these things had been done while his mind was closed in, remembering but not understanding, living in the agony of the past and blissfully, serenely unaware of the present. . . .

Suddenly the file clattered to the floor. Roland swayed and leaned against the bench for support, his nerveless hands hanging by his sides. He looked at M. Pinaud, and the agony and the fear in that fixed regard seemed to stir in the depths of that vacant emptiness like stones at the bottom of deep water.

"My mother," he said softly, "she is dead—do you know? She died today."

"Yes," replied M. Pinaud gently, his cigarette smouldering unheeded between his fingers, "I know. I was there."

"She died—and I could do nothing. That is why I came out here. There was nothing I could do, so I came here to work."

"That was probably the best thing you could do."

"When I am working with my hands everything is all right. When I try to calculate, the figures and the paper seem to mix. Black and white together, and the whole thing turns grey—and the greyness spreads and becomes huge—and I see those men again—standing there without heads . . ."

Suddenly he buried his face in his hands and stood there, leaning against the bench, his body racked with convulsive choking sobs.

In two strides M. Pinaud was at his side. He placed an arm around the slender shoulders, and his grasp was strong and friendly and comforting.

One of the doors banged with a sudden shattering violence and Marie Capt stood before them.

She wore a housecoat and her dark hair was unbound, flowing loosely down to her shoulders, framing the pale oval of her features. In their pallid intensity her eyes seemed to blaze as she spoke.

"What are you doing here, M'sieu Pinaud?"

Her voice was shaking with a taut fury she could hardly control.

M. Pinaud removed his arm and took a step away from Roland. His features were impassive but his eyes were troubled.

"I am investigating, mademoiselle," he replied quietly.

"Have you no sense of shame—no sense of decency at all? You know what happened here today. Can't you let us in peace even for twenty-four hours?"

M. Pinaud fumbled in his pockets, his eyes never leaving hers.

"I am sorry, mademoiselle," he replied, and the calm strength of his dignity seemed something against which the girl's anger could only break and shatter impotently. "You know I am sorry. I have already expressed my sympathy. But in spite of my regret and my sorrow my work must go on. I am concerned with facts. I am investigating a series of murders."

"That is no reason for you to come here at this time of night, spying on my brother, trying to trick him—to trap him."

"No."

M. Pinaud voice rang clearly and loudly, with a sudden authority that cut off her flow of hysterical words as suddenly as if he had clapped a hand across her mouth.

134

"That is not true," he went on quietly. "You know that is not true."

Roland took two steps forward.

"You are wrong, Marie," he said. "You are wrong and he is right. He has been kind. He is one who understands——"

His voice ceased suddenly, abruptly, as if the very utterance of the word had brought new problems to his mind, and for a long moment there was silence. Marie stood with her head bowed, looking at the floor.

M. Pinaud's groping hands had finally found his cigarettes and his lighter. The rasp of the flint broke the spell.

Marie looked up, and there were tears in her eyes.

"I am sorry, M'sieu Pinaud," she said simply. "Please forgive me."

For a long moment he stood there looking at her, his features impassive, veiled behind the swirling smoke of his cigarette. Only in his eyes that strange troubled expression still lingered.

She was so incredibly, so wonderfully beautiful. And she was so young—far too young to be mixed up in an affair as horrible as this. They were both young—like children who had been forced to grow up too quickly. And like children they would remain, once this horror had been expunged from their lives, for many a long year, while he who was a middle-aged man with a family would grow older and older until soon he would be an old man. He would be old while she was still young.

That was the reason why he had no right to look at her in that way, why he had no right to the thoughts and the desires that surged unbidden and spontaneously into his mind every time he looked at her; that was why his expression grew strained and troubled when he met the compelling frankness of her eyes.

All these things happened to you in the past, he tried to tell himself. You are now another person. And yet was that true? Was he not the same person, with the same thoughts and the same desires, who looked at life with a little more experience and a little more wisdom and perhaps a little more bitterness—but who remained fundamentally the same, in that he had the same nature and the same temperament as he had always had . . .?

And so he was a middle-aged detective engaged in doing the work for which he was paid, and she was the sister of his chief suspect. And yet was there not more to it than that, so much more, so much that was wonderful and beautiful and unattainable, and precious with a dream's exquisite fragility . . .?

M. Pinaud sighed, dropped his cigarette and ground it out beneath the heel of his boot.

He was Pinaud, the celebrated and already famous detective, engaged on a case which would soon add to his already remarkable reputation. He was Pinaud, a family man, the father of two affectionate and yet undeniably plain daughters whom he loved very dearly. He was Pinaud, and in his bed at home was the pleasant and amiable stranger with whom he had once been madly in love. He was Pinaud, and before him stood this girl, her dark hair unbound and the tears still glistening in her eyes, whose very look and inflection of voice and slightest movement could set his pulses racing as madly and as dangerously as if he were a boy of twenty. It was all very confusing and perhaps a little bitter and a little sad. . . .

He cleared his throat.

"There is no need to apologize, mademoiselle. Your

feelings are perfectly natural. If I were you I would go to bed now. It is late and there is nothing more to be done. I will see you tomorrow. Good night."

In the moonlight her features were a pale wonder of beauty. M. Pinaud stayed very still, in an attitude almost of reverence at her loveliness.

"I had to see you again. I had to see you before you went."

"Why?"

"To—to apologize once more, and to thank you."

"You have already done both, mademoiselle. There is no need to do so again."

M. Pinaud's voice was gentle and infinitely kind. He had been about to enter his car when she came running down the drive. Now he shut the door again firmly and leant his back against it.

Something hard between his shoulder-blades—something tangible—something real—to offset the moonbeams and the moonlight on her hair and the moon's clear cold radiance that seemed to drown in the sorrows of her eyes.

"Why should you do all this for us? What makes you do so much . . . for people you have never seen before?"

Something hard and reassuring behind him—steel and iron and beaten panel, drop-forging and casting and turning, metal shaped and moulded and hammered and bent to man's desire, metal obedient and responsive in a power that gave life to the design on a board—something to hold on to in the magic and the mystery of that silent night, whose beauty reached out in such an infinite embrace that the place in which they stood seemed to extend, wider and wider and deeper and deeper, until it became the whole world and they were the only two in it, standing there in

137

the silence, standing alone together enfolded in the magic and mystery, alone in the shadows that laid dark hands on the moonlight. . . .

Gently M. Pinaud placed his hands on her shoulders and turned her around.

"Look," he said quietly, "there before you is one reason."

Marie Capt looked to where the dark bulk of the Château surged beyond the trees, sleeping beneath the vast pale spread of the sky.

"What do you mean?"

"I mean that I can still remember a house like that, although with each year that passes my memories grow more dim, until sometimes they seem only like the awareness one has of a half-forgotten dream."

"You mean—you lived once . ."

"Yes, in one very similar, although much smaller. I remember a covered passage-way that led to the church, because in the time of Henri of Navarre they pulled down the convent and built a house over the cellars. I remember the vine whose stem was thicker than my body. I remember the funerals and how the sun hid the faces and the very sky seemed to weep with me, with tears of rain."

He felt her shoulders move under his hands, warmly and convulsively under the thin robe and nighthown, and he dropped his arms suddenly, as if in fear.

"Yes, I can understand that reason," she said simply.

"There is another reason, too," M. Pinaud went on, talking quickly in order to destroy those images which were still in his mind. "I remember other things far more vividly. I remember being cold and tired and hungry, and I remember a building with seven floors, and each floor was partitioned off with match-boarding into three, so that

138

three families could occupy the space meant for one, and I remember how through the thin matchboarding one could hear——"

He felt her hand, cool and soft and vital, against his mouth.

"No—no!" she whispered. "No—that is enough!"

For a moment he stared blindly past her at the house, and then he took her hand in his own.

"Yes," he agreed heavily, "that was a bad reason, but it was a strong one. It has been with me all my life and it will remain with me until I die—the fear of injustice and the hatred of cruelty. Against those I know I must always fight. And I had other reasons, too."

"Tell me."

"No."

"Tell me."

Soft and insistent her words in the moonlight, soft and seductive the parted lips and the dark eyes, eager and compelling, alive in the pale beauty of her face—how could he tell her all that she had come to mean to him, when he dared not admit it even to himself?

"No," he heard himself saying slowly and eavily, "not now, do not ask me now. Perhaps when all this horror is over and you are better—perhaps I can come back then and see you again."

"I wish you would. Perhaps then I shall find the words to tell you how much you have helped me."

Abruptly, M. Pinaud turned and wrenched open the door of his car.

"You had better go now," he said quietly. "It is late, and I still have much to do. Good night, mademoiselle."

Chapter Eleven

DR. REUGE lived in the beautiful white house beside the church. A light was shining from behind one of the lower windows as M. Pinaud rang the bell.

The doctor himself opened the door.

"Why M'sieu Pinaud——!" he began, his astonishment evident in his voice.

"I know it is late. I am sorry to disturb you, but may I come in?"

"Of course."

Dr. Reuge opened the front door wide.

"I have only just come in myself, but I am afraid my housekeeper enjoys earlier hours. Come this way."

M. Pinaud went through the hall into a very beautiful room. Standing with his square-toed boots planted firmly on a deep crimson carpet, he eyed the gleaming white-panelled walls and the rich mahogany furniture with an appreciative and all-embracing glance.

Having done this, without haste, he looked at the doctor, who was standing in front of him.

"I have just come from the Château," he said slowly and heavily. "I shall have no option but to arrest Roland Capt. I have found out how he did it."

"No!"

The doctor's ejaculation was incredulous.

"Yes—he tried to murder one of my detectives an hour ago. He probably thought he was eliminating me."

"But—but that was when I left him. No—wait a moment—it was longer than that. . . ."

The doctor looked at his gold automatic wrist-watch.

"Yes," agreed M. Pinaud. "He said you had left him half-an-hour before. Would you care to come with me now and see how these murders were done? I know it is late, but tomorrow there will be many things to do."

"Naturally. I am most interested. Have you come in your car, or shall we take mine?"

"Mine is outside. It will only take a few moments."

He was strangely silent as he drove the few kilometres to the Château. At the crest of the rise he switched off his engine, coasting in silence to the disused gatehouse.

"There is no point in waking up Mademoiselle Capt," he explained. "She has had a trying day."

The Château slept, a shadowed mass in the moonlight. Soon, treading quietly, they came to the back and the open window.

The body of Charles Valin still lay motionless exactly where M. Pinaud had left it.

Dr. Reuge turned towards it.

"Let him be," said M. Pinaud quietly. "It is only a faint. I will come back for him later."

Then he stepped forward and lifted the blade from the sill. Dr. Reuge felt its edge with his finger and muttered to himself. Then he laid a hand on M. Pinaud's arm.

"Look," he whispered, "we want to be quiet—there is a lot I want to ask you. Come back with me and have a drink and we can talk without being disturbed.

"Very well."

M. Pinaud lowered the blade very carefully and slowly and then led the way back to his car.

Once again they stood in that beautiful room, or rather

M. Pinaud stood while the doctor paced up and down restlessly.

"It is surprising," he said, "and yet it should occasion no surprise; it is perfectly natural. It is just the sort of contrivance he would have assembled—simple and ingenious and effective. A release cord to the wall, you said, where he could wait in the shadows. I wonder how he got them to look in."

"I don't know," replied M. Pinaud quietly. "Perhaps he did not have to; an open empty window space is enough. I did not have to be told. But then I was curious. Perhaps he had to induce them to look. But it does not matter now."

"No, the method is not important. We know that it succeeded. He could have forged that blade—as he forged the gates."

Suddenly he stopped his pacing and faced M. Pinaud.

"But he is not responsible for this."

"Indeed?"

"No. Do you know who is responsible?"

"Who?"

"Those who sent him to a war when he was nineteen—those who wasted the years in making fortunes out of concrete fortifications—those who sent ill-trained and badly equipped soldiers against tanks and dive-bombers."

"Morally you are right. Legally he is the one responsible."

"Maybe, but that is not his fault."

"He might do it again."

"Yes, I see what you mean. He will have to be confined, I suppose—for life. . . ."

"Probably. There is reason for mercy, as you say."

For a moment there was silence, and then the doctor struck his brow.

"I completely forgot. I asked you to have a drink. Excuse me."

He walked to a cabinet beside the tall french windows, which were partly open, lifted the lid and took out a bottle and glasses. Over his shoulder, without turning round, he spoke casually.

"Did you see anyone when you were there, by the wall?"

"No. I did not need to."

Dr. Reuge swung round.

"What do you mean?"

"I mean that I know who was there—just as well as you know, M'sieu Reuge. I know who is the murderer— just as you know. And we both know that it is not Roland Capt."

M. Pinaud's voice was perfectly calm, almost expressionless, but as he spoke each quiet word, so the tension began to mount, almost palpably, in that quiet and beautiful room, until the very silence seemed to quiver between them.

For a moment M. Pinaud allowed that silence to hang heavily in the air. Then, without the slightest change of expression, he reached inside his coat and drew his revolver from its shoulder holster. He held it loosely in his hand, but still he did not say anything and still that tension mounted and increased, assuring and threatening, like a living and an angry and tangible thing.

Then Dr. Reuge set the bottle down with a sharp sound and it seemed as if a spell were broken.

"I do not know what you are talking about," he said coolly.

"No?" replied M. Pinaud, still in that quiet and almost expressionless voice, standing there squarely, indomitably, with the revolver held loosely in his hand. "Then let me try to explain. Take a country doctor who is obviously living beyond his means . . . a three-carat diamond engagement ring . . . a car which although obsolete still needs a fortune from a connoisseur . . . this beautiful house——"

"I have my own money," interrupted Dr. Reuge. "I am not dependent on my income."

"You mean you had your own money, before you squandered it all. You need not trouble to lie. I had a certain amount of difficulty with the manager of your bank, but in the end he decided that it would be wiser to let me examine your account."

Dr. Reuge left the cabinet with a glass in his hand and sat down in an armchair. M. Pinaud waited for him to make some comment, but as he did not speak he continued.

"And so we have a doctor who is desperate for money, so that he can continue to live in the style to which he is accustomed. And there, right in front of him, on his very doorstep, is the Château Capt with all its income from its farms and its forests and its vineyards. What a prize for a country doctor!"

"I think you are mad, M'sieu Pinaud," said Dr. Reuge. "I have no idea what you are talking about."

M. Pinaud continued as if he had not spoken.

"And who stands in the way of this ambitious scheme? Only an old lady and a defenceless young girl and a boy who has given his health and his sanity and the best years of his life to undo the work of traitors and politicians. Only these three.

"But then someone else came blundering in. Just when you had everything organized, Pinaud appeared. And because you thought that Pinaud might be dangerous you did your best to get him out of the way. And that is were you made your mistake, M'sieu Reuge. Pinaud is not one to be eliminated. He is not to be disposed of in the most convenient way. When he is engaged on a case he stays there until the end. Other and better men have tried your tactics—but I am still here."

"I can see that you are here," replied Dr. Reuge patiently, "but I still have no idea what you are talking about."

"The night before last the innkeeper Dubois did his best to make me drunk and then tried to murder me. But it did not turn out quite as he had planned. His was the head that hit the flagstones of his cellar—not mine."

"That is just a tale. You were probably both drunk, and he lost his balance."

M. Pinaud looked at him for a moment in silence and then, almost imperceptibly, nodded his head.

"Yes. That is what you would say. And if I had been killed, that is what everyone would have said—even the *Juge d' Instruction.* That is what made the whole thing so diabolically clever. But I was not killed, and your friend the innkeeper, he did not die immediately."

"That is a lie."

"How do you know?"

"People who crack their skulls on flagstones usually die at once."

"Maybe they do. This one did not. He lived a few moments—long enough to talk."

"Nonsense! The ravings of a drunkard."

"Yes," sighed M. Pinaud slowly and heavily, "that is

145

what everyone would say. You picked a good tool for your dirty work. He was a drunkard. But what drove him to drink—what made him a drunkard in the first place—so that you could buy him—so that your money could put a price to murder?"

Again for a long moment, there was silence in that silent room. The sincerity and the indignation in M. Pinaud's quiet voice made his words cut like a whip. Dr. Reuge did not answer.

"About the poison in my food there is nothing to be said. You probably took good care that no one saw you come in or go out. Your attempt failed, and so it is only your word against mine. Fortunately, it is not the same with regard to the other matters."

"What do you mean?"

"Your filthy scheme had at least the merit of simplicity. The mechanics of that window would present no difficulty to an amateur engineer. Oh, yes, I took the trouble of investigating your career most thoroughly. Besides, you had access to Roland's forge and workshop when he was not there, or perhaps you even persuaded him to help you with some of it. That would be the kind of refinement of cruelty which forms part of the same pattern.

"You had no compunction about murdering two innocent people, neither of whom had injured you in any way, so that suspicion could fall on Roland. M'sieu Minoton must have found out something, so that you had to murder him to keep his mouth shut. And if anyone else had been here in my place, Roland would have been arrested and you would have been the first skilled and impartial witness to make sure that he was put away.

"And the *Juge d' Instruction* would tap his head significantly and mutter 'Shell-shock' to his clerk, and every-

146

one would think it sad that a legacy of the war should linger in such a dreadful way. Unaccountable fits of violence, poor fellow. Lock him up—or at least confine him somewhere where he cannot get out in case he does it again.

"Oh, you are clever, M'sieu Reuge—clever in a way that makes me sick with disgust. But this time you will find that your cleverness has taken you too far. This time you have tried your filthy tricks on Pinaud, and this time they have not worked. None of them have worked—and Pinaud is still here, standing with his muddy boots on your beautiful carpet, and for the first time since he came to Chassagne he understands what has been going on here.

"That was the chief obstacle—the heir to the Capt fortune," continued M. Pinaud, still in that same and equable tone. Indeed, throughout the whole of that interview he hardly raised his voice. Perhaps that was what made his whole attitude the more terrifying, that and the air of implacable ruthlessness which stamped his every gesture and his every word. Perhaps it was that air of certainty, that sense of conviction that seemed to arm him like a shield which kept Dr. Reuge sitting in his chair, unable to find the words either to deny or protest.

He could only sit there and listen to that inexorable voice, as level and as restrained and as passionless as doom.

"After the trial you would have had no difficulty in declaring him legally insane, and the estate and the income, in due course, could then be legally yours—after your wife had signed a few papers."

Here, in spite of himself, his voice trembled slightly.

"I do not know what you have been persuading her to take—a doctor has so many opportunities—but of this

I am certain. Once you are out of the way, her illness will not last. She trusted you. She took whatever you gave her. The old lady had more sense. She was shrewd enough to suspect; she preferred to endure the pain. And her love for Roland kept her mouth shut; that is why your plan was so fiendishly clever.

"But she refused to take what you had carefully prepared for her, and so you had to find another way. The abscess in her ear provided a golden opportunity, and Antoine on the roof was her sentence of death.

"Who suggested that it was about time the roof was repaired, M'sieu Reuge? Was it the old lady, racked with pain and tortured with worry about her son? She had other things to think about. Was it Marie, whose only thought was how to get well and feel alive again? Was it Roland, who in all probability never even considered that the Château had a roof at all?

"I should think it was the good doctor, the friend of the family, the fiancé of the daughter, the companion of the unfortunate heir, who suggested that it was about time Antoine was summoned to mend the roof."

The doctor's face had grown deathly pale, but his voice was still strong and resonant.

"You have no proof—you are just making wild accusations."

"On the contrary, I would never make such an accusation without proof. You could not allow such an opportunity to go by. The crucible was outside, on the balcony. You only had to ask her to sit still while you fetched the warm oil to put in her ear. She just sat there and waited—probably with her eyes closed, because she was suffering and in pain.

"Dr. Vinet performed an autopsy on her body this afternoon. He found the pellet of lead in her skull."

Chapter Twelve

M. PINAUD looked at the magnificent bookcase which took up most of one wall. Behind the small leaded panes of soft blown glass the leather-bound volumes gleamed richly in the light, brave with their gold lettering, dignified in their repose.

M. Pinaud shifted his feet on the luxurious pile of the carpet. He felt out of place amidst all that beauty, lonely in the majesty of that graceful room. Each one of those volumes would probably have paid his salary for a month. He felt out of place and he knew that he was out of place, that he did not belong there, that his world and the world of Dr. Reuge were two worlds that would never touch.

And yet he continued to stand there, with his hands still dirty and earth-stained as a result of his efforts in the garden, and tired with the deathly and almost sickening fatigue of reaction and shabby in his cheap and ill-fitting suit—a poor picture in such a splendid frame. Weariness had etched deep lines into his features and their strength glistened with perspiration and set into the hardness of stone.

He continued to stand there, and in the implacable determination of his attitude there was a dignity and a majesty that transcended his whole person and invested him with a power and an authority that seemed to stand before him like a sword.

Dr. Reuge sat perfectly still in his armchair, balancing his glass on his knee. When the tension of that silence seemed to stretch almost to breaking-point, M. Pinaud's quiet voice eased it again.

"You spoke just now about proof. There is some more which may interest you. To cut the release cord and to hide successfully in the shadow of that very old and dusty wall, one would have to crouch very close to the vine. Roland, as you know, usually wears a white shirt. Tonight, when I spoke to him, I took care to examine his shirt very carefully. It was spotless. He obviously could not have cut the release cord. Neither could he have entered the house from the barn to change it, or else I would have seen him."

M. Pinaud's hand went into his side pocket.

"Your coat is dark," he continued calmly, "and would blend well with the shadow of the wall. This is what I removed from the shoulder of your coat as I held the door open for you to get into the car."

And he held out something between his finger and thumb. It was the broken skin and crushed pulp of a squashed grape.

Dr. Reuge looked at M. Pinaud's hand. Then his gaze travelled up to M. Pinaud, standing there indomitably, implacably, the revolver held loosely and yet with assured competence in his other hand.

Suddenly his pallid features contorted into the ghastly travesty of a smile. With incredible speed he hurled the glass he was holding right in M. Pinaud's face and with almost the same movement he was up from his chair and

150

out through the french windows, which yielded to the sudden savage thrust of his hand.

The glass, of heavy crystal, caught M. Pinaud on the temple, momentarily stunning him. The wine splashed in his eyes, blinding him. Nevertheless, he managed to fire two shots, but in the circumstances it was not surprising that his aim was wild.

Fiercely he rubbed his hand across his eyes. There was both blood and wine on the palm. Holstering his revolver, he paused only to bind his handkerchief tightly around his brow, and then, disregarding the pain, he dashed out in pursuit.

As he came across the lawn to the front of the house he heard the roar of the Bugatti's engine, and even as the tail-lamp shot off down the road he was running as fast as he could towards his own car.

And so began that amazing drive in the moonlight—a drive of such fantastic horror that for many a year afterwards M. Pinaud would awake at night shouting in terror as he relived, in the vivid imagery of a nightmare, the risks he deliberately took on that memorable night.

He knew that the car in front was faster. He knew that Dr. Reuge was guilty; his flight was an admission of guilt. He knew as well that if Dr. Reuge escaped his whole case would collapse.

Therefore he could not let him escape. It was quite logical and comparatively simple. The only difficulty lay in the fact that his car, although fast, was no match for the Bugatti.

Nevertheless, M. Pinaud was a logical man. He saw what he had to do, and thankful that the issue was at least a simple one and uncomplicated, proceeded to do it to the utmost of his ability.

He had one advantage. His car had front-wheel drive and therefore he could corner faster than the other machine. Also, he told himself grimly as he sent his car roaring along the white road, he would make himself another advantage—he would drive better and faster and more skilfully.

And so the two cars raced through the lovely moonlit night, beneath the serene pale arch of the sky which seemed to mock their fantastic speed with the tranquil vastness of its immensity. and always the huge car thundered on ahead and always the other car roared along behind, losing on the straight and gaining on the curves and corners, holding the road like a train on rails, with M. Pinaud's eyes intent on that flying ribbon of white which the low bonnet seemed to wind up beneath it, his head a little to one side listening to the pulse and the beat of the racing engine.

Through deserted villages they fled, bouncing and shuddering over badly laid cobbles, screaming around bends and tearing down the straight tree-lined road, past moon-washed walls of stone which streamed past M. Pinaud's shoulder in a pale white line, beneath the dark black shadow of the poplar trees and out again into that pale unearthly radiance shed by the moon as it drifted and swam, lazily, remotely, ineffably high above them, across the floating clouds in the sky.

And in M. Pinaud's head, throbbing with the pain of his wound, beat the endless refrain of the roaring exhaust and the powerful whine of the engine, a continual and reverberating echo which seemed after a while to be resounding inside his brain.

Beneath it all there flowed an urgency which would not be denied, which seemed to make it even worse—he must go faster—faster—faster; he could not afford to let him get away—he must take chances—he must beat him—he must not let him escape.

The road began to climb and wind. The Bugatti had more power, but the bends were dangerous and the huge car was difficult to manœuvre. Dr. Reuge was forced to slacken speed.

And M. Pinaud began to gain. With screaming tyres he flung the low car into the bends, judging distance and estimating speed with consummate reckless skill, taking chances time after time to gain a few seconds at the risk of his life and driving like a man inspired.

Now he had no time to think. He had no time even to be afraid, because his mind was fully occupied. He had become a machine, calculating and estimating and deciding with automatic precision.

The car seemed endowed with a life of its own. He felt as if he were guiding something that was alive, powerfully and frenziedly alive, and its eyes were the two headlights that sent a golden swathe of radiance ahead, cutting the shadows with a warm and comforting glow.

The whole world was contained in that swathe of light before him and the road that unwound so swiftly into it and all that fled and raced by on either side—the ghostly blur of stone walls, the sombre black shadows of the trees and the tall sleeping houses that caught the roar of the engine and the crackle of the exhaust and flung them back into his throbbing head, deafeningly, maddeningly, stridently.

And still, slowly and yet inexorably, M. Pinaud gained.

He braked for a town and snaked through the narrow

deserted streets and screamed around the corners and out again into the tranquil vastness of the open country. On one side, for an interminable distance, ran a high stone wall, the boundary of some estate.

And then he saw the cart.

The red light of the Bugatti had roared on, and one second there was the golden road in front of him and the next there was a great cart, piled high with baulks of wood. The horse seemed to have come from the field and was heading diagonally across the road towards the wall.

There was no one leading it. Head down, tugging and straining at the heavy load, the horse was obviously making its way to that side of the road to which it was accustomed.

There was hardly time to think. In a second M. Pinaud had jammed on the brakes. And in the same second, even as he put them on, he realized that he could not stop in time, not at the speed at which he was going.

The gap was closing. To hit the wall or the cart at that speed would be the end. And he did not dare run off the road. Too often it was raised on a causeway, higher than the level of the fields. If he risked it he would probably overturn.

As he thought he acted. He took his foot off the brake and flattened the accelerator on the floorboard. The car seemed to leap forward. M. Pinaud took it as near to the wall as he dared, praying there were no jutting or overhanging stones. The horse flung up its head and reared high in the air as he shot by literally under its hooves— and he was through.

There was no time even to think of the narrowness of his escape. The Bugatti had drawn away. M. Pinaud began to take chances once again.

Vaguely he felt that perhaps he ought to pray. It seemed unfair to take such risks and expect the good God to look after him without having made at least some special plea. But even as the thought came vaguely through the noise and the throbbing in his head, he knew that he could not do it. He could only hold on to that wheel with all his strength, while every thought, every emotion, every nerve in his being were all concentrated only into the task of keeping the car on the road.

Gradually, relentlessly, he regained the distance he had lost.

Now, after a particularly winding stretch of road, he was right behind the Bugatti, and for a while the two cars roared on through the night like two coaches coupled on the same train, moving in unison, curving, winding, roaring, climbing, turning in a harmony of motion that would have been beautiful to watch were it not for the mad and fantastic recklessness of their speed.

And then M. Pinaud put his finger suddenly on the steering-wheel ring of his electric horn and kept it there while he drove, faster and faster and closer and closer.

He knew how nerve-racking it would be. The noise did not help the throbbing in his head, and after a little while his own nerves began to jump in protest, but he kept his finger grimly on the ring, knowing what effect it would have on Dr. Reuge.

M. Pinaud knew that he did not have any hope of passing the Bugatti. But he also knew that Dr. Reuge could not be certain of that. He knew as well that the other's confidence had already been badly shaken, as in that car he must have been certain of a getaway. And when a man's confidence is badly shaken, his driving does not improve. And when to the strain and stress of driving a heavy car at a dangerous speed at night there is added the nerve-racking and uninterrupted inferno of powerful twin electric horns blaring just behind, a badly-shaken confidence is bound to be effected.

Coldly, calmly, ruthlessly, M. Pinaud reasoned it all out, driving faster and faster and sending the blinding glare of his headlights closer and closer through the rear window of the car in front.

Brilliantly, remorselessly, implacably, he kept behind the Bugatti, fighting a war of nerves that was terrible and almost awe-inspiring in its savage intensity.

And for those last few moments, aided by fate or chance or perhaps that destiny which sometimes tips the scales towards those who strain with every nerve and bone and sinew, the road wound and curved and dipped and climbed with never a straight stretch, and the Bugatti could not get away.

The great car lurched and swayed, skidded and re-covered as Dr. Reuge misjudged the turn. M. Pinaud accelerated to split-second nicety, pulling the car out of its drift with faultless precision. Under the blood-stained handkerchief the grim lines of his face seemed to set into stone. It would not be long now. Dr. Reuge's nerve had started to go.

And once it had started, the end was quick.

Over a bad patch of surface the back of the Bugatti bounced and shuddered and then suddenly skidded in the direction of the camber of the road. Dr. Reuge's reaction was too quick and too violent; his correction sent the car completely out of control. At the speed the car was travelling the pot-holed surface made it wholly un-manageable; the resultant skid was even more violent than the first and the car turned completely round, overturned and crashed into a tree.

M Pinaud took his finger off the ring, braked carefully, stopped the car and switched off his engine.

Then for a moment he sat there with his eyes closed, drinking in the peace and the tranquillity of the night, and above all the silence—the blessed stillness that seemed to flow into the very depths of his being with the slow and healing benediction and the cool and calming cleansing of some surging and majestic wave. To be quiet —to rest—to listen and hear nothing. That was all he needed. That and a little time. Time for the hard core of tension within him to unfold and relax—time for the trembling in his hands and the ache in his thigh to lessen and vanish—time for the glare to die in his eyes and the echoes from his mind and the aching rigidity of all his muscles to slacken—time to think and become normal once again.

Then after a while he lit a cigarette and walked back towards the wreck.

It is interesting to speculate, at this moment, as to what drove him to risk his life in this manner, not once but a dozen times. In his memoirs he makes no comment on that nightmare drive; the fact is mentioned, briefly and concisely, that the Bugatti was the faster car but that he succeeded in catching it. And that is all.

Perhaps it was his interest in Marie Capt, his admiration for that indomitable figure her mother, and his sympathy for Roland which provided the mainspring for his actions. To say nothing of his genuine and spostaneous liking for M. Minoton.

In all his numerous cases he had never identified himself

so strongly or so sympathetically with the protagonists as in this one, with the inevitable consequence that seldom had he felt so implacably ruthless towards the perpetrator of the crimes as now. In addition, the very cold-bloodedness of Dr. Reuge's plot, with its complete and callous disregard of all human decency, must have revolted him more than he knew for his reaction to have been so violent and so savage and so strong.

Now M. Pinaud stood beside the wrecked car, alone in the silence of the night. Dr. Reuge was dead, horribly and yet mercifully dead.

For a long time he stood there, alone with the dead man in the radiance of the moonlight, while all about him the earth slept and the peace of that vast silence seemed to reach down into the innermost depths of his being.

At first his thoughts were confused and strangely, poignantly bitter. He had succeeded. Once again the great Pinaud had triumphed. The doctor's flight had been positive vindication of the truth of his accusations.

And yet who was to blame—the doctor himself, or the father who had accustomed his son to such a life of luxury that he could not face the thought of doing without it? Or the conditions that had kept him operating in the war, as he had recounted, for sixteen hours at a stretch, without rest, without anaesthetics, without facilities? Could a man survive such an ordeal unaffected? Could a man remain wholly and completely sane after such an experience?

M. Pinaud sighed and buttoned his jacket. Suddenly he felt cold. Perhaps this way was better. At least, Dr. Reuge had not suffered. His death had been quick and merciful. His thoughts ran on and on.

He thought of Charles Valin, lying there in the garden of the Château in a dead faint, oblivious and heedless of the drama which had just been enacted. In time he would make a good detective. His nerves would harden like tempered steel after a hundred more such escapes. His courage and calmness would increase each time he heard the beating of the wings of Death. His fortitude and endurance would sharpen on the whetstone of experience.

In time—if all these things happened to him—he might even become a great detective. He had taken the first step, even if he was unconscious. Perhaps it was just as well. One could not have the climax of a case cluttered up with detectives. Someone had to be in charge. One hand was sufficient at the helm. Otherwise how could credit be assigned where credit was due?

He thought of Marie Capt and the wonder of her beauty in the soft silver sheen shed by the moon and the dark shadows deep in her eyes that not even the moon's liquid light could brighten, and the magic and the wonder of her presence that transcended even as it implemented the magic and the mystery of the night.

He thought of M. le Chef's acid comments regarding expenses when he had asked for Dr. Vinet to take a plane, as it was imperative that he reached Chassagne without delay.

Other and even more important people are compelled to conduct their daily activities and limit and control the extent of their journeying with the assistance of trains, which were run most efficiently, competently and reasonably by a special Department of the State for that very purpose. Why then, should Dr. Vinet disrupt an organization which was already functioning with the greatest efficiency, to reach an obscure town some few hours earlier? What difference could it possibly make? How unreasonable and exacting could some people get? No doubt M. Pinaud would like nothing better than for him to have an army of men at the *Sûreté*, ready and waiting—doing nothing, mark you—just sitting on their behinds and waiting—and incidentally drawing their pay—just waiting for the summons that would isevitably come from M. Pinaud as he leapt into action on his next case . . . and so on and so forth. Thus M. le Chef.

M. Pinaud had replaced the receiver gently in the middle of it. Sometimes these provincial connections gave a lot of trouble.

Now he sighed again, at the memory of the narrow-mindedness and bigoted pedantry that always seemed to clutter up the topmost *echelons* of any large organization, and hoped that Dr. Vinet would find a pellet of lead when he finally arrived by train and performed the autopsy tomorrow.

If he did sot—well, it did not really matter. The body of the doctor in this shattered wreck was sufficient proof that once again M. Pinaud had been right.

His hand went to his side pocket and he pulled out the bunch of grapes he had picked from the vine. Most of them, having been in his pocket, were crushed and squashed. Absentmindedly he began pulling off the sound ones and eating them. Their flavour was delicious.

Now that you have finished this book you will probably be interested in other best-selling CONSUL BOOKS obtainable from all newsagents, bookstalls and bookshops. Published by World Distributors (Manchester) Limited, 36 Great Russell Street, London, W.C.1.